# Resurrection Point

by

**William Blackwell**

**Resurrection Point**

This is a work of fiction. Names, characters, businesses, places, events, and incidents are either the products of the author's imagination or used in a fictitious manner. Any resemblance to actual persons, living or dead, or actual

events is purely coincidental.

Cover design by Telemachus Press, LLC

Published by Telemachus, LLC

Paperback ISBN: 978-1-997835-01-1

Version: 2017.12.29

# Acknowledgements

Heartfelt thanks to my loyal and supportive readers, friends and family, the hardworking staff at Telemachus Press, and my editor. Special thanks to The Government of Prince Edward Island for its financial support.

*Black draperies, likewise in the gloomy room, shut out from our view of the moon, the lurid stars, and the peopleless streets—but the boding and the memory of Evil, they would not be so excluded. There were things around us and about of which I can render no distinct account—things material and spiritual—heaviness in the atmosphere—a sense of suffocation—anxiety—and, above all, that terrible state of existence which the nervous experience when the senses are keenly living and awake, and meanwhile the powers of thought lie dormant.*

—Edgar Allan Poe—*Shadow—a Parable*

# RESURRECTION POINT

# Prologue

Byron Solstice trudged down the street in the dead of night, a faraway sliver of a moon barely illuming his path. Something wasn't right. He knew it was coming, could feel it really—a sense of dread that invaded as a small knot in his stomach and twisted like a hissing snake through his throat. Now it was constricting his chest as he moved—causing his breathing to come in short, panicked gasps.

He stopped, frozen by a metallic click echoing from a doorway. He fought to push the serpent back inside his stomach or cough it out like an unwanted chicken bone. He coughed for a second, cleared his throat and felt better. But not much.

He was terrified.

A dark figure emerged from the doorway and machine gun fire—short, shrill staccato-style bursts—cut through the silent night, shattering the eerie calm.

Byron sprinted to a nearby building—the setting was surreal, like an abandoned western-style ghost town. But the ghosts were coming out to play. He dove behind a gray run-down saloon, skidding along the dusty dirt as a trail of bullets punctuated his provisional escape.

He waited, slowly trying to control his labored breathing, searching his extremities for injuries. Satisfied he hadn't taken a hit, he crawled to the building's corner. The enemy stopped firing.

He searched around and saw it—an AK-47 machine gun right in front of him. He picked it up, taking comfort in the

4

feel of cold steel on his sweaty palms. He poked his head around the building and saw the dark figure again—this time charging forward and growling like a wolf.

He stood up instantly, machine gun leveled, as the dark hooded figure with its fiery red eyes and shark-like fangs came closer. He stepped out and fired—three short and uncontrolled bursts that struck the enemy multiple times in the head and across the chest.

The enemy ran about twenty feet from inertia before dropping to the ground, groaning and twitching for a few seconds before finally dying.

Byron continued down the barren streets of the forgotten ghost town. About fifty feet later another dark figure emerged, announcing itself with a threatening sneer and fire-glowing eyes. Byron took no chances. He opened fire and cut the beast down, not even bothering to watch him die.

He had no idea where he was. But it was obvious he had to get out of here. And, like some macabre video game, the object was kill or be killed. And he didn't want to die. At 42-years-old, he was much too young to die, still had many goals he wanted to achieve before he came knock, knock, knocking on death's door.

He trudged on. In an instant, he saw a four-legged, wolf-like monster, baring its formidable fangs, rushing forward. He leveled the world's most popular killing machine and plugged it full of bullets. It lost its footing, fell, and skidded along the road, howling and then whimpering before falling silent.

Byron continued on. *Three down. How many more to go?* He didn't know.

A side street came into view and he took it, thinking his journey, whatever it meant, wherever it was supposed to lead, would be easier to complete off the main drag, off the path of his attackers. He moved along stealthily in the darkness, the diffuse light from the moon barely guiding his way.

The street was lined with old, abandoned, decrepit buildings, houses mostly, with a smattering of small businesses in the mix—a barber shop, a coffee shop, a small café.

Some of his fear had left, the recent kills serving as a confidence booster. Maybe he could get out of here, reach the end game, whatever it was. *Kill or be killed.* He knew he had to keep going, couldn't stop or he would be overrun by monsters.

He strained his eyes to see ahead. A small yellow light shone in the distance from a window of an old two-story house. As he got closer, he could see some movement inside the living room, barely discernible through the faint glow, but there nonetheless. He saw black arms waving frantically.

He stopped dead in his tracks. The door flew open and dark creatures—some charging on two legs—others on four, stormed out and attacked en masse. He sprayed the wave of attackers with bullets and one-by-one they dropped dead, a few cut down within a few feet from where he stood. They screeched, hollered and whimpered as they died—a bloody massacre of gargantuan proportion.

As the sound of the last round of bullets slowly echoed and was swallowed by the night, so too were the horrific screams of the dead and dying.

Once more, all was silent. And black.

A thought crept into Byron's mind and slowly formed. *I'm dreaming. This is a dream.* The realization brought a smile to his face, a twinkle to his green eyes. He ran a hand through a thick mop of wavy brown hair, gazing around at the other buildings. He was sure he was dreaming. And, since that was so, how about a few more kills? Play the game. Win the game. May as well have some fun. No damage can be done anyway.

He walked on.

Monstrous beasts, fiery red eyes, slowly poked their heads from buildings, advanced and he cut them down joyously with the machine gun, really getting into his role, the sound of the weapon, the horrific screams of the dying. He was impervious. He would wake up and everything would return to normal.

He felt like he had been thrown into a larger than life amusement park shooting gallery. He couldn't wait to get to the end to claim his prize.

Strolling down the side street killing everyone and anyone, he couldn't have been happier. Then something happened. His machine gun jammed. He fidgeted with the trigger and realized he had no idea what he was doing. Other than a pellet gun, he had never handled a firearm in his life, let alone a Kalashnikov.

He heard a faint roar from behind. He spun around and stared wide-eyed in horror. His victims, riddled with bullet holes, slowly picked themselves up, dusted themselves off. They roared in symphony, a blood-curdling hellish sound, and marched purposefully toward him.

*What? I killed them. How can they be resurrected?* Then another thought crept into his mind. *Is this a dream? But it must be. This shit doesn't happen in real life.*

The creatures rushed him en masse, slamming him hard to the ground. In an instant, they were on him, biting large chunks of flesh, tearing piece by piece. Growling and devouring. And he could feel the excruciating pain. It was real. He tried to scream, opened his mouth, but no words emerged.

*I'm dying.* He felt the life draining from his body, darkness take hold, and then there was nothing at all. Nothing but total blackness and no comprehension of anything.

Dead.

Abruptly, he jerked, tumbled out of bed and landed hard on the oak hardwood floor. He slowly picked himself up, waiting for his heart rate to slow.

Akila stirred, rolled over and went back to sleep. He stared at his motionless girlfriend.

He was so terrified. He thought if he moved, he would have a heart attack, the sound of his thumping chest so pervasive and forceful.

He wiped a sweat-soaked forehead and waited, glancing at the clock: 2:56 am. Finally, his heart rate slowed and he stripped off his sweat-soaked underwear and t-shirt, replacing them with clean and dry ones.

In the living room, he sat down on the couch in the darkness and stared at a large unlit television screen for twenty minutes before returning to bed. He tossed and turned for two hours before falling into a restless and fitful sleep.

Byron had no idea how profoundly real and frightening his nightmare would become. When he finally woke, the details were indistinct—only a dark and ineffable feeling of doom and despair lingered.

# Chapter One

"If you linger long enough, you'll buy it," Byron told Akila.

"Maybe I want it," Akila Bartley said, a twinkle in her deep green eyes.

Byron knew Akila well enough to know that if she wanted something bad enough, she would just buy it. Working as a public relations officer for city hall, she could certainly afford it. It wasn't a hint. But, if she really loved the little gold necklace they were looking at in the small jewelry store on Kent Street, Charlottetown, PEI, wouldn't she love it even more if Byron bought it? And, then, every time she wore it, felt it around her neck, or looked at it, wouldn't she remember him? He thought so, knowing the associations people make with gifts seldom evaporate. It was almost a form of Pavlovian conditioning. Hear a song, see or touch a sentimental gift and you think of the person associated with it.

But, in this case, he knew it would be good. She drove him crazy. They were in love.

"I really like it," she said, holding it to her neck as she brushed away a lock of long, wavy blonde hair. "What do you think?"

The gold necklace had a small dolphin that smiled as it leaped in the air. Don't dolphins always seem to be smiling?

Byron tried to avert his eyes away from her curvaceous breasts, the generous cleavage the green V-neck short-sleeved blouse afforded. But he couldn't.

"Not my boobs, the necklace. I know you like *them*."

"I love them."

"I love dolphins," Akila said with an infectious smile.

"Do you know the dolphin was an early Christian symbol?" a middle-aged shopkeeper said, approaching from behind with a warm smile. She pushed horn-rimmed spectacles up a long, pointed nose.

"No, I didn't," Akila said.

"Yes. It was a symbol for resurrection. Are you religious?"

"No," Akila said. "I'm very spiritual though."

The shopkeeper smiled again.

Byron took his cue. "How much is it?"

The woman adjusted her horned-rimmed spectacles again, ran a hand through her gravity-defying beehive hairdo and extended a hand. "Can I see it?"

Akila handed it over. She examined it briefly. "This is an 18 carat gold Spiga chain. The dolphin is so cute, isn't he? This is regularly $249.95 but it's your lucky day. Guess what?"

"It's on sale," Akila offered.

"It is indeed. Today, August 11th, is the last day of the sale. It's only $199.99."

"I'll take it," Byron said, wondering if he refused would he be dragged into a back room for a good-cop-bad-cop close.

Akila beamed. "You're buying it for me?"

"Of course, honey."

She hugged him, planted a wet kiss on his lips as the saleswoman returned to the cash register.

"Now I'll never die—and if I do I'll get resurrected," Akila said, holding the smiling dolphin and kissing it as they left. Outside, they stopped and Byron put it on Akila's neck and fastened the clasp securely. It glittered.

"A good luck charm," Byron said. "It's beautiful."

Akila nodded and smiled.

The bright sunshine warmed Byron's bones. It felt so good to be outdoors after spending the last few months cooped up inside his home office hammering away on his ninth novel, ironically, a story about resurrection. Was it possible for art to mirror reality? He thought so but he didn't care right now. He knew he and Akila had the next month off—they were officially on holidays.

And, that ninth work, *Resurrected Souls,* at least for the time being, had been put on the back burner.

An independent writer, or indie author, he had been immersed in his work for the last eight months, cranking out a novel a month. Although he loved reading, and supporting fellow indies, he had been so immersed in his own projects he hardly had time to do anything else. He was either doing editing passes, cover design with an artist trying to render his vision, last-minute proofs on formatted manuscripts, or creating a new novel.

And of course there was the social media marketing: Pinterest, Tumblr, Twitter, Facebook, Goodreads, to name a few of the websites Byron used for book promotion. As an indie author, to be successful, you had to remove the author hat for at least half a day, don the marketer hat and go to work promoting—a tough and, at times, daunting task.

At least it had become that way for Byron after eight months working eleven hours a day for six days a week. He had finally hit the wall—was physically and emotionally spent. Writer's burn-out. Done. Cooked. Fried. Toasted. Exhausted.

Last week had been spent entirely in his two-story home in Charlottetown, mostly sleeping, eating, drinking, answering

Mother Nature's call. He was manic about his writing and it had taken an enormous toll. Migraine headaches, once unfamiliar, had inflicted debilitating pain toward the end of the push and on some days handicapped his creativity for long stretches of time.

At first he didn't recognize the symptoms. But, his doctor insisted he take time off work or suffer the consequences—a heart attack or complete nervous breakdown.

Even his publisher had told him enough was enough. The company couldn't process the books as fast as he could write them. He had been told to take a break, spend some time with his girlfriend and revisit the creative process with a fresh and rejuvenated mind in a month or so.

But Byron couldn't complain. His efforts had finally resulted in monthly sales that averaged around $2,000, generated by eight titles—all in the horror genre. And he had no illusions about wanting to be rich, even a best-selling author. He wasn't greedy. If he could earn a respectable income, his work could educate, influence and entertain then, hell, he was happy. If he could afford to continue to create—follow his heart's passion—then he figured he was doing much better than most people, not that it was a competition in his mind either.

They had no mortgage on their home. Akila earned $55,000 a year, so how much did they really need? *Be thankful for what you've got. It could disappear in a New York minute.*

As if on cue, a maroon Quattro A6 ran a red light at an intersection.

Akila quickly grabbed Byron's arm and yanked him back on the curb as he dazedly ignored a flashing *DON'T WALK* sign. "Get back here. Are you still in a daze?"

That's all she had time to say.

She was interrupted by the loud crash of glass breaking, screeching tires skidding too late, a loud metallic clang as the two vehicles collided. The Quattro slammed into a newer gold Ford Fiesta with such force it careened across the intersection for about fifty feet before grinding to a stop, steam and water from the ruptured radiator spewing like a geyser while smoke from the damaged engine swirled.

Byron heard screams, horns honking and saw the twisted mass of metal, formerly two dependable automobiles.

Without thinking, he rushed over to the Fiesta as crowds gathered, Akila following close behind. She darted to the Quattro.

Byron tried the passenger door as he looked in. It opened. His eyes widened in horror at the bloodbath of carnage in the driver seat. His friend, Elias Masters. *Oh no, that's Elias!* The Fiesta had been T-boned, the driver side mashed on impact. The air bag had inflated but it didn't matter. The force of the blow had crunched the driver door, crushing Elias in the process. His blood-soaked head lolled to one side. His skull was crushed almost beyond recognition. His right eye, wide open in shock, the other eye unrecognizable. His mouth contorted in terror.

Dead on impact. He never had a chance.

Akila managed to pull a door open on the Quattro and struggled, now with the help of some bystanders, to free the driver. She smelled smoke. Where there was smoke, there was fire.

Byron raced over and joined three people pulling on the unconscious Quattro driver, a middle-aged businessman in a black suit. As they dragged him along the pavement, close to the curb, it happened. A small flame quickly snaked across the Quattro hood, a second later a large boom thundered as it exploded into a ball of flames, ignited the Fiesta and then it flared with a reverberating boom, raining debris everywhere , a huge fireball fanning into the sky with a whoosh.

Byron ran to the curb, tackled Akila to the pavement and covered up as panic-stricken pedestrians screamed and ran for their lives.

His best friend had just met an untimely death, his body burning in a fiery metal casket.

Byron slowly stood up as the flames subsided, grimly staring at the burning vehicles. How could that be? Elias was dead.

At that moment he wanted more than anything in the world to have his friend back.

# Chapter Two

"He's not coming back," Akila said later that evening as they sipped red wine at home. "He's dead."

Byron had told her about an eerie feeling he had after giving statements to Detective Clay Redmond—a feeling that Elias would be coming back. Even though his rational mind told him it wasn't possible, he couldn't shake the visceral vision of a smiling Elias, standing atop a tower on a bright and sunny day, waving—the same silly grin, mop of curly blonde hair, blue eyes, the casual surfer-dude look of his laid-back friend.

But the vision had evaporated as soon as it had materialized and now details of it were sketchy. Where was the tower? What kind of tower was it? Was this an actual vision or was it merely a symptom of a grief-stricken mind trying to cope with the loss of a dear friend? Byron didn't know, and he wasn't about to try and figure it out right now.

His months pounding at the keyboards, churning out novel after novel, had left him with brain drain. Lucky, Akila was an author in her own right and had published a suspense romance novel, or she might not have understood his addiction to writing and might have been less patient with the long hours at the keyboard. As it was, however, it had put a small strain on the relationship. Toward the end of the eighth month, Byron could tell by her demeanor that she was feeling neglected. He had noticed it first about ten days ago, after finishing a long and exhaustive writing stint.

He had gone into the kitchen for a coffee refill, the elixir that fuelled his fire, and saw Akila sitting at the table, reading a book, the corners of her lips pulled down slightly, almost in a pout. He had asked: "Are you reading a depressing book?"

To which she had replied: "No, actually it's a positive, upbeat story."

At that point he realized it. He had been paying way too much attention to the characters in his mind and not nearly enough attention to the love of his life—living vicariously through the heroes of his books at the expense of his relationship—retreating into the familiar comfort of his colorful imagination while she suffered.

Returning to his keyboard—he just had to finish that last bit—he had decided it. "When this is done, I'm done," he had said out loud to no one in particular, not realizing he didn't have any choice in the matter.

He finished the horror novel, crashed and burned.

So, after a week of recovery, they had agreed to take some time off and rekindle their romance. He had been careful, even while immersed in the characters of his books, not to let the deep bond they had developed become completely unglued. The glue might have lifted just slightly, separated from the surface a tad, but he felt he could cement it back permanently with the right amount of tender loving care.

And right now, other than the recent devastating tragedy, and a few haunting flashbacks from the resurrection nightmare recently, it was foremost on his mind—rekindle the fire.

The rest will follow. Or wait.

It always does.

"You're right," he said, sighing. "But I miss him."

Akila sat beside him on the black leather couch watching flames dance in the fireplace. She sipped her wine. "So do I. Don't forget he was my friend too."

He inched closer, put a hand on her leg, caressing it softly. "I know. Let's try and forget it for now, okay?" He couldn't control the urge for carnal pleasure.

She nodded, took his hand, and searched his eyes. "Okay."

"It's the first day of our holidays and, in spite of what happened, I want to make it memorable."

He kissed her softly on the lips and she pulled him close with desire. The kiss continued. Through the cotton fabric of the white studded blouson tank top she wore, he watched her nipples grow erect. She wasn't wearing a bra. That drove him crazy. He crawled on top of her, embracing in a passionate hug. How long had it been? He didn't even remember.

*Damn shame, considering I'm lucky to have a goddess for a girlfriend.*

In a matter of seconds, he had lifted the top over her head and fondled her breasts, teasingly licking and kissing her nipples. It didn't take long before she grabbed him by the hand, said "bring your glass," grabbed the bottle of red wine and led him upstairs, where they made passionate love for over two hours.

Finished and smiling, they cuddled together on the king-sized bed, staring out at the full moon shining through the sheer blinds of the bedroom window.

A few minutes later, Akila drifted off to sleep and Byron's mind raced. He would never admit it, but while making love to Akila, a glowing white image flashed in his mind. He thought about it now, trying to retrieve it from some obscure compartment, recognize it.

Five minutes later, nothing materialized. As he shifted his thoughts to their holiday plans, it struck him like a lightning bolt—East Point Lighthouse.

# Chapter Three

Constructed in 1847, East Point Lighthouse is located in King's County, PEI, on Cape East Point. 1989 marked the last year the sixty-four foot octagonal-shaped white tower was manned. Currently automated, it serves as a navigation aid for both deep sea and offshore fishing vessels. Beside the lighthouse, a fog alarm building has been converted to a café and gift shop. The seasonally-operated tourist attraction offers guided tours.

But guided tours were the last thing on seventy-eight-year-old Riley Fitzgerald's mind that night as he worked in his welding shop a few short miles from the lighthouse. His late wife, Eleanor, had already seen enough of the historic lighthouse when she was alive. After all, he was the caretaker and had a key. They would often sit in the lantern room as the electric light swirled and cast its intermittent glow far out into the convergence of the Gulf of St. Lawrence and the Northumberland Strait. They found the view mesmerizing, the warning beam hypnotizing.

But those peaceful evenings gazing out at the ocean, the twinkling stars and the moon were now a distant memory for Riley. His wife had abruptly died two weeks ago from an undiagnosed brain aneurism that had ruptured in her sleep.

Only problem was, Riley didn't want Eleanor dead yet. He wanted her back.

He finished the weld on the metal handle, slid the welding mask up over his thick gray hair and regarded his effort. The line was straight, the weld solid. "That's a damn fine weld."

Sonora, his black cat, stirred from her sleep on the hood of the old 1957 Chevrolet Bel Air Convertible, raised an eye briefly and closed it again, finding familiar comfort in her lazy slumber.

Riley pulled the mask off, set the MIG gun down on the welder and killed the power. He walked through tools strewn on the grease-stained concrete floor over to the small window that had a single fan blowing the toxic smoke outside. Glancing at the sleeping feline, he didn't know how she did it, but she was always by his side, even if it meant sleeping through toxic smoke and fumes. He coughed, adjusted fan speed up a notch and as an afterthought pulled a remote out of his pocket and pressed the button. The double garage door whirred up and the remaining fumes slowly dissipated. *Why didn't I do that before instead of welding in this smog?*

Sonora opened one eye, craned her neck momentarily, and returned to her nap after the mechanical whirring noise stopped. She had seen it all before.

Riley coughed a few times and returned to his project—a metal dolly. He was almost finished. It was almost time, but not quite. First he had a man to see, and it wasn't a man about a dog.

It was a man about a resurrection.

A few minutes later, shaved and showered, he sat at the wheel of his trusty Chevrolet C10 pick-up. The dark green work horse had served him well over the years and he never tired of driving it. He glanced in the passenger seat, noticed the LED flashlight, fired up the engine and disappeared down the driveway, the moonlight and twinkling stars faintly illuming an otherwise black night.

About ten minutes later, he pulled off Lighthouse Road into a parking lot, brought the truck to a stop and killed the ignition. Exiting, he raised his arm to his face, turning up the collar of the green jacket, shielding himself from the buffeting wind. He hadn't bothered to check the weather forecast. He didn't need to. He could tell by the aching in his knee joints, an unwelcome but reliable weather forecaster. A storm was brewing. Things were going to get real ugly real soon. He would have to make it quick.

He unlocked the door to the octagonal tower and entered. Guided by the flashlight beam, he slowly climbed the stairs, uninterested in the historical lighthouse artifacts, photos, pictures, even signatures of shipwrecked survivors scrawled on the white walls. It was old news to Riley and he had a singular purpose—to resurrect Eleanor. He just hoped he could conjure up the apparition of the man who had promised it would become a reality.

He stopped on the third level, catching his breath momentarily before shining the beam around the room. The tower, marked by pediment windows, had five levels including a lantern room at the top from which the beacon shone intermittently 24/7. The suffused gray moonlight shone through the window and cast an eerie glow on Riley's bulky frame. The room was sparsely furnished with a cot-style bed, sleeping mannequin, a wood-burning stove, a wooden desk with a chair and a few oil lanterns—relics of a bygone era of manned lighthouses on PEI.

"Samuel, are you there?" Riley sat down on the single wooden chair, still breathing heavily from the climb. The wind whistled and the old tower creaked, its antique bones straining under the powerful force.

He waited in silence a few minutes before deciding. "Ahh, to hell with it." He extracted his metal flask, unscrewed the top and took a long pull, the strong taste of Lamb's Navy Rum burning his esophagus on the way down.

But it warmed and comforted him. And took the edge off, which is what Riley wanted right now. This whole resurrection thing was starting to creep him out. For the first time, he wondered if he should even go through with it.

He screwed the top on and returned the flask to his jacket pocket. *Don't overdo it tonight. You have to talk to Samuel. You don't know him well enough to talk to him drunk.*

"Samuel, I need your help here."

Silence.

He shone the beam around the room, hoping the large dancing circle would awaken Samuel, whom he had come to view as a savior. "Samuel, where are you?"

Silence.

He adjusted his horned-rimmed glasses, sliding them up his nose so the Coke-bottle lenses were closer to his beady blue eyes.

Thunder boomed and lightning cracked out at sea, the bright forks snaking down, slicing through violent waves rolling shoreward. It had yet to reach the peak of its fury but was already announcing itself angrily, the intensity of the wind increasing and the rain, now coming in sheets, pelting the old tower.

*Should I leave? Forget the whole thing?*

He absently trained the flashlight beam on the ceiling directly above him. Without warning, as if answering his thoughts, a silver apparition emerged from the light, floated down and stood directly in front of him.

Riley had become lost in the fond memory of his late wife and didn't immediately notice it. He was just about to reach into his pocket for another swill of liquid confidence when he heard it.

"Where is she?" the booming voice of Samuel Longhorn said.

Riley jumped in the chair, dropping his flashlight. It clunked on the wooden floor, rolling in a circular fashion before finally settling to a stop on the uneven surface.

"Who?"

"Your wife, who do you think?"

Riley's hands started trembling. His eyes followed the black boots, red pants, black cape. Samuel's grimacing face came into view, emerging from the silvery mist. He had a thick red beard, a pointed nose and black—was that possible?—slits for eyes. A black Davy Jones pirate hat trimmed with gold completed the swashbuckling appearance.

A dark feeling permeated Riley's body and mind.

He didn't know the man's history or agenda—was too afraid to ask, actually. Maybe that information would come in due time. And maybe it wouldn't. But, on the two previous conversations he had had with Samuel one thing had become abundantly clear. Samuel wanted to resurrect Eleanor from the dead. Riley thought he heard mention of a few others that Samuel had on his resurrection list, but now he couldn't be sure. The death of Eleanor was too recent, his grief much too heartfelt to be able to process information reasonably. The only thing that was clear was that he wasn't prepared to part with Eleanor just yet. He couldn't imagine living another week without her around. And this man had promised to bring her back.

So, for now, he wouldn't ask too many questions; just follow instructions, as he had been doing to this point, knowing that soon he would hold his beloved wife in his arms.

"Eleanor?"

"Yes—Eleanor."

"She's buried. I haven't had a chance to ... retrieve her yet. But I've made the dolly. It's all ready. I'll bring her tomorrow night."

"Bring her tomorrow at midnight." Samuel stepped toward Riley, knelt down on one knee and slowly brought his intimidating face to within inches of Riley's grizzled mug. "And don't be one minute late."

Riley jerked away from the acrid tobacco and whiskey smell that assaulted his nostrils. *A ghost with vices.* "I won't be late. Don't worry—will she be the same—I mean when she comes back to life?"

The pirate scratched his thick beard, pondering the question for a moment. "She won't be the same."

The darkness tightened. "She won't?"

"No, she'll be much better than before."

"Better? How so?"

"Time will tell, old man. Not everything at once."

# Chapter Four

"Not everything at once. You'll see it in due time. Keep your eyes closed," Akila said. She stood behind Byron, covering his eyes with both hands. He couldn't see anything.

He grabbed her hands playfully. "I want to see."

"We're almost there." She guided him down the hallway, finally stopping in the kitchen. "Okay." She removed her hands and he blinked, adjusting to the late morning sunlight beaming through a kitchen window.

"What?"

"Over there, on the table."

He searched the table, scanning the vase of fresh-cut roses, the decorative wooden salt and pepper shakers, two vinyl placemats displaying pastoral beach scenes. "You bought me flowers. That's sweet." He spun around and kissed her playfully on the lips.

Akila smiled. "Not just that, silly. Take another look."

He searched the table again and saw it; a small black velvet jewelry box, almost obscured by the dark oak table top. "What's that?"

"Open it."

Byron opened it. Inside was a gold necklace with a smiling dolphin, a symbol for resurrection as he had learned, and the identical gift he had bought Akila. He smiled. "That's sweet baby. Thanks. I love it."

They kissed.

She gently withdrew from the embrace. "I just thought you'd like one. That way we can be matching—a celebration of our union."

"And we don't have to worry about dying. If we do we'll be resurrected."

Akila laughed that infectious and melodious laugh that so drove him crazy.

Byron laughed too. But then he remembered his vision just before dozing off last night and his boyish countenance turned somber. His best friend was dead. And he wanted him back.

Akila's sunshine-smile slowly faded, feeding off his emotion. "What's wrong?"

"Nothing. Well, actually I ..."

But before he could tell her how much he missed Elias, her cell phone rang. She answered it. "Hello ... Susanne, how are you?" A frown slowly creased her soft features as Susanne talked.

Byron knew it wouldn't be good. Susanne Watterton was Elias's girlfriend of three years. And now he was dead, plucked away from the living at the young age of thirty-five by a careless driver who had run a red light. Dead before his time, while the driver recovered in hospital with what Detective Redmond called "non-life threatening injuries." It remained to be seen if the man would be charged with criminal negligence causing death, but it could result in both a criminal and civil court case. Surely Susanne, whose meager salary as a salesperson in a local gift shop wouldn't sustain the house mortgage, would be hunting for blood money.

Akila palmed the phone's earpiece. "She wants us to come over for a while."

Byron expected it. Akila had spent an hour comforting Susanne on the phone last night after she had identified the body. He had overheard part of the conversation, something about Akila offering to "check in on you tomorrow to see if you need anything."

They were good friends, after all. It was the least Akila could do.

He nodded and she lifted her palm from the earpiece. "Give us half an hour." She hung up.

Twenty minutes later they arrived in Akila's blue Quattro A-6. Byron wore the gold dolphin—a good luck charm, or so he hoped.

It was a bright sunny afternoon but their spirits were dark—deflated by the tragic turn of events. Akila parked and they stared in silence for a few minutes at Susanne's modest three-bedroom bungalow on a quiet residential street in Charlottetown. The sea-blue wood frame house had white wooden shutters casing the windows. Pink tulips decorated the small porch and the modest front lawn was neatly manicured. They had just bought it a year ago, were planning to marry and start a family—have at least two kids.

Akila searched Byron's green eyes for some strength. "I know Elias was your best friend, but, baby, let's try and keep this as positive as possible. Misery only breeds more misery."

"You're my best friend, baby."

"You know what I mean. Best male friend."

Byron scratched his nose and adjusted his black-rimmed glasses. He had a lump in his throat and his stomach was in knots. He burped, and with the escaping gas, felt the acidy taste of vomit squirt into his mouth. He swallowed hard and winced. It stung his esophagus on the way down. "Okay."

The color drained from his already-pale skin. It was only a few days ago he had met with Elias for lunch at a diner near McCain Foods, a potato processing plant in Borden-Carleton, where Elias had worked as a supervisor. He remembered it as if it were yesterday. To the busy chatter of blue-collar workers, they munched on cheese burgers and fries. Elias's deep blue eyes twinkled with joy as he wiped a bit of catsup from his chin, smeared it on a napkin, ran a hand through his thick blonde hair and declared: "I'm going to marry her. She's the woman of my dreams. I can't stop thinking about her. I'm going to ask her tonight, but keep it a secret, okay?"

Byron had promised, grinned ear-to-ear and offered a heartfelt congratulations. If he could ever get his mind off writing, he was planning the same thing with Akila.

"You don't look so good. Are you all right?" Akila asked.

He inhaled deeply and exhaled slowly as the happy memory of Elias faded into nothingness.

"Just felt a little sick to my stomach. It'll pass. Let's go."

Susanne, her wavy brown hair disheveled, hazel eyes bloodshot from crying, greeted them at the door with a feeble attempt at a smile. She wore a long white cotton nightgown with pink roses. She had yet to meet with a hairbrush or a shower. Evidently grieving superseded domestic chores or personal hygiene. Who could blame her?

They hugged and she led them into the kitchen where they sat down.

"I'm just sick about this," she said. "Do you know Elias proposed to me the night before last?" She didn't wait for an answer. "We were just starting to plan our wedding ... we were going to tell you guys about it today over dinner and drinks here. We talked about a family, how many kids we were going to have ... the whole nine yards and now this. Snatched away by that bastard who T-boned him. That fucking bastard who wasn't paying attention, was probably drunk for all I know, comes along, runs a red light and blows my fucking boyfriend up. I could barely recognize the body. If it weren't for a few scars that didn't get burned to a fucking crisp I wouldn't have."

"I'm going to make some tea," Byron said, while Akila put a consoling arm over Susanne's shoulder. "Anyone want some?"

Akila nodded and Susanne continued ranting, her eyes welling up with tears.

"Well, if that driver thinks I'm done with him, he's got another think coming. Can you believe it, his name is Bryce Smith? What kind of a name is Bryce Smith? Sounds like a fucking John Doe. But who's stuck with the John Doe now? I'll tell you who, it's me, that's who. Elias has become John Doe. Unrecognizable. John fucking Doe. My future husband—John fucking Doe!"

Her monologue trailed off, she covered her face with her hands, propped elbows on the wooden kitchen table, and cried softly, her sudden angry outburst supplanted with grief and sorrow.

Byron placed a teapot of caffeinated tea, along with sugar, milk, spoons and cups on the table and sat down watching his girlfriend comfort Susanne. He didn't know what to say so he said nothing, only poured the hot liquid slowly into white mugs.

"Have some tea," Akila said, standing behind her friend, both arms wrapped around Susanne's chest. "It'll make you feel better."

A few minutes later, Susanne had wiped away her tears with a paper napkin and looked a little more composed.

Akila sat beside her while Byron occupied the head of the table.

They sipped tea.

"You tried to save him?" Susanne asked Byron.

Byron nodded, the lump in his throat making slow ascending progress. He gulped his tea and swallowed hard trying to force the acidy liquid down. "I tried to, but he was dead on impact, trapped in the car. There was nothing I could do."

"Thanks for trying."

"He was my best friend."

"I know."

"We all loved Elias," Akila said. "He had one of those special personalities that instantly lights up a room. And his sense of humor and practical jokes—he could lift anybody up if they were feeling down."

"I've been getting phone calls all day from his friends and coworkers," Susanne said. "Everyone at McCain's has been great. Even my boss told me to take as much time off work as I need."

While she talked about specific comments from friends and family, to the nods and approval of Akila, Byron thought about how he could divert Susanne's attention away from this terrible tragedy. At the very least, perhaps he could show her some hours of enjoyment, so she wouldn't become obsessed over Elias's death and slip away into a black abyss of terrible depression. Of course she would have to go through the grieving process—would have to do that largely on her own and in her own mind. But, at least, as close friends, surely he and Akila could show her some of the happiness and joy they had experienced as two couples hanging out.

He felt sure Elias would have wanted that.

"Why don't we go for a picnic today?" he said on an impulse.

Susanne stopped in mid-sentence. There was a faint flicker of excitement barely detectable in her mesmerizing eyes. She loved the outdoors. "Where?"

"I don't know, how about East Point Lighthouse?"

"East Point Lighthouse?" the women asked, almost simultaneously. "What's there?"

"There's a great picnic spot, a great beach nearby and the lighthouse is supercool. I've been doing some reading about it lately. Have you guys ever been inside?"

They shook their heads.

"I read that lighthouse actually received a distress signal from the Titanic."

# Chapter Five

The Titanic. A sinking ship. *Is that what I am? A ship on its maiden voyage about to strike an iceberg, sink to the bottom of the ocean and die.* Byron didn't know, so he swallowed hard, trying to push the sinking feeling into his stomach, where it might be devoured by stomach acids and thus flushed from his system. He was conscious he wore a frown, a tragic symbol of his loss. Not wanting to bring his friends down, he made a conscious effort to smile, even a straight line redolent of a dead-pan expression would be better than a frown.

He caught his reflection in the car mirror and thought the look came off more of a wince, the pained expression people display answering Mother Nature's call while squatting on a toilet. He sighed. It would have to do for now.

Akila drove, Susanne in the front passenger seat, while Byron sat in the back glancing at the pretty scenery abundant on the island. The women chatted and his mind wandered aimlessly while he glanced around, hoping the greenery, the infinite vistas out to sea, and the clear blue sky would brighten his spirits.

*Why did I suggest East Point Lighthouse? Because you had a vision, that's why. It holds the key to Elias's heart.* He pushed the thought from his mind. They were almost there, on Lighthouse Road, just passing Diligent Pond. On the way out they had stopped at KFC, picked up a bucket of chicken, some coleslaw, macaroni salad, fries and, for good measure, two bottles of dry white wine and a twelve-pack of beer. Even though public drinking was illegal on the island, Byron didn't think anybody would mind. At this time of the year most of the tourists had gone home anyhow. He knew Susanne could use a sedative of sorts. Hell, they all could.

They pulled up to the scenic cape of East Point Lighthouse. There were six other cars in the parking lot and Byron knew that at least half of them were probably for staff employed at the café, gift shop and lighthouse. They found an isolated parking spot beside the red cliffs that gave way to the expansive ocean views. It was a calming, almost surreal view. A young Japanese couple occupied a picnic table. Tourists. The woman leaned against the picnic table, posing seductively and smiling. The man snapped photos with a digital camera.

A man in worn blue coveralls walked around the park-like lawn with a litter-spear, stabbing bits of debris, depositing them into a green plastic garbage bag.

He smiled at them, avuncular, as they exited the vehicle.

"Beautiful day," Akila said as they stretched in front of the car and took in the pastoral views.

"It is," the man said, approaching. He was heavy-set with a thick gray beard. He wore a black baseball cap that partially concealed bushy gray eyebrows. Thick horn-rimmed spectacles framed his grizzled face. He set the spear and garbage bag down on the picnic table, pulled off the baseball cap and wiped a sweaty brow, swiped a hand on the coveralls and extended it.

"Name's Riley," shaking Byron's hand with a firm grip. "Riley Fitzgerald."

Byron made introductions.

Riley offered hearty handshakes and warm smiles. Byron and Akila took in the view while Susanne chatted with Riley.

"You here to tour the lighthouse?"

"We are," Susanne offered.

"Magical powers, that lighthouse."

"What's that?"

"There's more inside there than meets the eye."

"What do you mean?"

"If you have a sixth sense, you'll feel it."

"Feel it?"

"Let me know when you come out. You'll see."

There was a moment's pause. Riley's eyes darkened suddenly and he stared into Susanne's hazel eyes. "Is your last name Watterton?"

She knew what was coming and frowned. "It is, why?"

"I read about Elias in *The Guardian*." There was real concern etched in his face. "They mentioned your name as his fiancé. I'm real sorry about that."

An uncomfortable silence followed.

"I'm sorry to bring it up. I didn't mean to upset you. I just lost my Eleanor ... I know it's not easy. But she's coming back tonight. Tonight's the night."

The conversation had caught the attention of Byron and Akila. They returned to Susanne's side, Akila with a protective arm around her friend's shoulder.

Susanne wiped her eyes. "What are you talking about anyway?"

"I'm sorry. Maybe you're not ready. But, when you are ... look me up. My name's in the book." Riley offered a conciliatory smile, fetched his accoutrements, turned and lumbered away, methodically stabbing pieces of litter that were scattered few and far between. He glanced back. "You all have a good day now."

By the time they opened the door to ascend the stairs of the lighthouse, Susanne's mood had darkened. And Byron had no idea why, but something the old man said rang true. He pushed the thought from his mind and focused on cheering up Susanne. Akila's arm had returned to her friend's shoulder.

"What's he going on about anyway?" Susanne asked as the red door creaked while swinging open. The lighthouse was dead quiet. Only the distant chirping of summer swallows and the gentle lapping of the waves was audible. No one else was inside.

"I wouldn't worry about it?" Akila said. "He's probably senile or something."

Susanne wouldn't let it go. "Tonight's the night? What the hell's that supposed to mean? Does he think he's going to resurrect his dead wife or something? Did she even die?"

"I think I saw the obituary a few weeks ago," Byron said, immediately regretting his words. The subject was clearly not brightening Susanne's mood—quite the opposite actually.

"You did?" she asked as they slowly ascended the sturdy gray wooden stairs.

Byron stopped, turned around, and nodded. "He's still grieving. I wouldn't pay any attention. It's normal for him to want her back. She's not coming back. You're listening to a mind sick with heartache and grief." He wasn't doing a good job of consoling Susanne. And he didn't believe half of what he had just said.

It was Akila who bailed him out as they reached the second floor and gathered around a red-cased pendant window to take in the view. "Listen, you guys, Elias would want us to enjoy the memory of his life, not wallow in grief. Can we drop this? He's not coming back."

"You're right," Byron said, noticing Riley had stopped collecting garbage and stared up at them. Byron didn't bother mentioning it, hoped they wouldn't notice.

Susanne nodded, worry and grief still etched in her brow. She looked straight out at the calm blue ocean waters.

Byron tried to lighten the mood. "I've got a direct line to heaven with my new cell phone. We can have a few drinks and drunk-dial Elias later—tell him we're drinking it off in his honor."

The women smiled.

Byron forced a laugh.

"What does drink it off mean?" Susanne asked.

"Well, you know if you get too drunk, you have to sleep it off? Well I just changed it around. If you get too stressed you have to drink it off ... drink all your troubles away."

"He's always messing with the English language," Akila said.

"I can see that," Susanne said. "But let's go to the beach after this and drink it off."

"Here, here," Byron said. "A woman after my own heart."

They viewed some of the old lantern covers, foghorns, oil lanterns, historic pictures of previous lighthouse attendants, other artifacts and ascended another floor, where they viewed the sparsely furnished bedroom in which lighthouse attendants once slept. A flesh-colored mannequin slept in a small cot by a window, partially covered by a thick wool blanket. The mannequin's vacant eyes stared at the wall.

"You think we should wake him?" Byron asked.

They smiled.

"Come on buddy ... get off your lazy ass and get some work done. The ships are coming."

The mannequin didn't move, not that they expected him to.

A minute later they reached the top level, where the electrically powered marine lantern slowly turned, flashing an intermittent beam of light. The circular room was walled with windows and the floor and ceiling were made of metal.

Byron gazed out at the calm waters, turning a dark gray due to a blanket of clouds that lazily floated shoreward. A housefly buzzed on the inside of the glass, struggling futilely to escape. The insect would probably never get out. And did it really matter, with an average life expectancy of between two weeks to a month. *Maybe to him, but not to me.*

After a few minutes enjoying the view and commenting on some of the well-known landmarks, they started their descent. Byron didn't know if the women had felt it but a cold chill suddenly crept up the back of his neck as he started down. He shivered, following them down the stairs. They picked up their gait, seemingly in a hurry to leave.

They were ahead of him when they reached the room that served as a bedroom. As they descended, Byron suddenly stopped. The mannequin. Something was wrong. Its movable head had been turned away from the wall and pointed at the ceiling. Its flesh-colored eyes stared eerily upward, the wool blanket pulled down, revealing its naked plastic chest.

"Are you coming?" Akila said, halfway down the stairs.

Byron started at the familiar voice. In an instant, he decided not to say anything. He had already opened his big mouth without regard for the word discretion and managed to upset Susanne.

He wasn't about to push it.

"Coming," he said, trying to sound calm—even though he could feel his heart thumping rapidly.

# Chapter Six

Climbing into the pick-up that night, Riley was conscious of the quickened and irregular palpitations of his heart. It wasn't often he exhumed dead bodies. This was a first. He reached for the silver flask, emblazoned with a fiery dragon—a gift from his late father, God rest his soul. He unscrewed the cap, took a nip, enjoying the numbing effects of the rum warming his stomach, and sat for a few minutes staring out at the full moon high in the sky. The recent storm had given way to calm, clear conditions. At least the weather was cooperating.

He breathed deeply for a while until he was satisfied his heart had returned to normal, or at least something approaching normal. There wasn't anything normal about what he was about to do.

After he had finished work, he had spent the day cleaning the kitchen in the old two-story home and preparing items he planned on cooking for his wife—a surprise dinner of sweet corn on the cob, pork chops, baked potatoes and a special rhubarb sauce with vanilla ice cream. It was Eleanor's favorite dessert. It was the rhubarb sauce that had taken the longest, heating, stirring and adding just the right amount of lemon juice and brown sugar. Too much and it's too sweet—too little, too tangy.

But Riley had followed one of Eleanor's recipes to the letter, tasted it just before leaving, savored its tangy-sweet flavor and turned the propane stove off, making sure to cover the large pot so the taste of the sauce would titivate with age.

He smiled, imagining how Eleanor's face would brighten when she sat down to dinner. Usually it was she who did the cooking. She would be delighted that Riley had taken the initiative. Hell, he even had a bottle of her favorite red wine, a vase of cut red roses, matching floral-patterned China, and two tall candles adorning the dining room table.

It would be a feast fit for kings and queens.

He started the truck and drove off into the night in search of her dead body. Soon after, he turned off Highway 16 onto Cemetery Road. Lights twinkled in the few homes that dotted the road leading to the cemetery. He hoped he wouldn't be noticed. He had a lot of work ahead of him. In his favor was the soft dirt that had only recently been shoveled over Eleanor's coffin. And he had will and determination. Come hell or high water, he was going to get his dear Eleanor back.

Creeping through the moonlit night with duffle bag, dolly and flashlight, Riley arrived at the fresh gravesite, removed the wreaths, flowers and cards, and began digging. He sweated as he worked, felt a throbbing pain in his back, but steadfastly continued, now running on a power-boost of fresh adrenaline. But soon, the adrenaline was gone—adrenaline dump. He labored and panted—old bones and muscles screaming a litany of protests. He ignored the pain, only stopping briefly to wipe a sweaty brow, replace his baseball cap, steal a nip of rum and carry on.

Exactly two hours later, the shovel crunched into the dark oak coffin. He paused, took a few deep breaths, and opened the casket. Eleanor's wrinkled face smiled up at him and he jumped, expecting her to speak. He returned his gaze to the object of his desire and realized her eyes were closed. At first glance, he thought they were open and boring into him. It was the fatigue. It must be. He took another nip of rum, climbed to the surface and extracted a long yellow nylon rope from the duffle bag.

He was about to slide down into the hole when something caught his eye—a luminescent white apparition, a wraith. A pirate resembling Samuel Longhorn strode past, not thirty feet away. Riley's eyes widened and he adjusted his spectacles to afford a better view. He thought he saw the man tip his hat and grin wickedly but then the image disappeared.

Without giving it a second thought, he slid down the hole, hoisted his lifeless waif of a wife up, wrapped some rope gently around her upper body and slung her over his shoulder like a sack of potatoes. He grunted and groaned, finally climbing to the surface where he tied her securely into the dolly in an upright position. Perhaps by some unexplainable reflex, Riley would never know, her eyes opened when he had her securely tied in place. He started, felt a stab of pain on the left side of his chest and stopped suddenly, breathing deeply for a few minutes until the pain subsided. It felt like the curtain of night was enveloping him. His vision blurred for a moment before he regained his composure, got a second wind, and began feverishly piling dirt into the hole.

An hour later, he had filled the hole, carefully replaced wreaths, cards and flowers, slung the duffle bag over his shoulder, and slowly pushed the dolly along in front of him, the full moon and flashlight guiding the way.

But there was one more light—or lighthouse—yet to offer its guiding light.

A few minutes later, he had Eleanor securely strapped into the truck bed and barreled down East Point Road toward East Point Lighthouse. Fear had seeped into his veins and he gripped the steering wheel hard, white-knuckled. He wanted to get this over with. Doubts were also creeping into his mind. *What the hell do I think I'm doing? Raising Eleanor from the dead? What would my pastor say?*

He pushed the thoughts aside as he reached Lighthouse Road, turned right and decelerated. In his anxiousness to get it over with, he had been speeding. He tried to calm his breathing as he caught sight of the beacon of light in the distance—for him a beacon of hope, a light at the end of a dark tunnel of loneliness, despair and grief.

He parked, exited the vehicle, climbed in the truck bed and slowly wheeled Eleanor down a makeshift plank and onto the gravel surface. He fumbled for his keys as he approached the door, the full moon casting an eerie glow on the surroundings. The door creaked open and he spun around suddenly. Was that movement in the gravel? Nothing.

He scanned the parking lot for signs of life. Nothing.

He unlocked the door, swung it open and quickly pushed the dead-body dolly inside, breathing heavily from equal parts panic and fatigue.

He rolled her into a corner, gently positioned the dolly upright and, flashlight beam guiding his way, lumbered over to the stairs and sat down to rest. He glanced at Eleanor, who regarded him stoically through open and unblinking eyes. *How the hell did her eyes open?*

Lines of moonlight seeping through windows cast a pale glow on her vacant expression.

Riley contemplated pulling the dolly up the three levels to the lantern room and winced, rubbing an arthritic right knee absently. It sucked growing old. He danced the flashlight beam on the walls and then trained the beam into Eleanor's eyes. They sparkled yellow as the light passed over.

Her gaze was fixed on Riley. And it was giving him the creeps.

He wasn't looking forward to the next task, lugging the dolly up three flights of stairs to the lantern room, where he was told the resurrection would take place.

He slid out the flask of liquid courage and took a long pull, hoping it would calm his rattled nerves. It helped, but only a little.

He checked his watch: five to midnight. Samuel had told him to be in the lantern room by midnight. But he knew lugging the body up the formidable stairs would take longer than five minutes, even though Eleanor only weighed a hundred or so pounds. The cumulative effects of bringing her to the surface, digging out and refilling the gravesite had taken its toll. His lower back throbbed with pain and other muscles he didn't even know he owned were offering a stinging resistance to movement of any kind.

He felt like collapsing on a couch, drifting off into an easy and restful sleep. But no, he couldn't. He had come this far. And he hadn't done all this work for nothing. He slowly stood, ignoring the protestations of his legs.

Four minutes to midnight. *Shit. Don't doddle, you idiot.*

A chill suddenly gripped him, starting in his lower back and shooting straight up to the nape of his neck like the tip of an icicle sword.

He looked up and saw it. Like an angel from heaven, a white misty apparition appeared and slowly floated down. As it landed, the shape became distinct, but not wholly recognizable. It vaguely resembled the wraith he had seen at Kingsboro Cemetery.

Was it his pirate friend? "Samuel, is that you?"

"Untie her," came the gruff response. There was no mistaking the voice. It was Samuel, his pirate savior.

Riley didn't ask questions. He quickly untied the ropes binding Eleanor and guided her body as she crumpled to the floor. He knelt down and brushed a lock of her curly gray hair away from her eyes and, for a second or two, admired her soft features. In death, as in life, she was beautiful to him—on the inside and the outside.

"Step away," Samuel said.

It happened as Riley stood up. A vaporous white mist swirled around the corpse, elevated it and slowly guided it up the stairs.

*Thank God. My work done for me.*

Riley was mesmerized by the sight of his wife floating away, followed by a trail of white mist. It was magical. His previous doubts and fears had all but disappeared. He knew Eleanor would soon return, his other half, soul-mate, friend, partner and, yes, lover. At his age, he had no problem getting it up—and without the aid of any prescription drugs, thank you very much.

The apparition of Samuel, Eleanor and the white mist disappeared.

Riley stared a few seconds before following. He wanted to see the resurrection. Flashlight beam guiding his way, he slowly ascended the staircase. As he reached the third floor, a high-pitched whistling sound stopped him in his tracks. The assaulting noise swirled around inside his head like a bullet does before exiting with deadly repercussions. He staggered from the ear-splitting pain, cupped both hands to ears and dropped to his knees.

But, in an instant the sound disappeared and the room grew quiet. Riley removed his hands, blinking as the pain slowly evaporated. He heard a clunk, looked up startled, and saw it. Or rather, saw her. It was the unmistakable black shoe of Eleanor, followed by a stockinged leg, a flowing black dress, then her entire body descending the spiral staircase that led to the lantern room.

She stopped, spun around and examined him quizzically. "I had the strangest dream. I died and went to heaven. But then you brought me back to life."

# Chapter Seven

The angry mob of beasts sprang back to life soon after Byron killed them—this time not a few minutes later as before. Their numbers had increased tenfold. And there was something else, something more terrifying. There was no place to hide. He was on a beach, somewhere in PEI, he presumed, but it was so dark he couldn't be sure. He remembered waking up on the sand and hearing noises: snarls, growls, ear-splitting screams of the dead and dying.

He stood up and saw the monsters, black furry animal-humans with demonically enlarged heads, some with big ears and still others with wolf-like and pig-like heads. Their eyes glowed yellow, orange, fiery red as they savagely ripped limbs from panic-stricken, fleeing human victims.

Was it a nightmare? Byron tried to wake up but couldn't. The moonlight barely silhouetted the carnage in front of him and he could hardly discern the victims from the monsters. He instinctively dropped to his knees, feeling in the sand for it. He knew it had to be here. It was in the last dream; the arsenal, the loaded AK-47. It didn't take long before he felt the cold steel of the reliable killing machine, the ammunition belts. He flung the belts over his shoulder, loaded the machine gun, released the safety and opened fire—short staccato bursts cut through the screams of the dying, the snarls of the monsters from hell.

One, two, three dropped dead with short, shrill screams. But seconds later, they were not only standing up again, they were attacking with a renewed quickness, vigor and rage, borne of a need for revenge.

They closed in on him, circling like a pack of wolves.

He saw a small opening in the circle, pointed the weapon ahead and squeezed off multiple rounds, the hail of bullets guiding him through the ever-tightening noose of death. He ran along the sand, his breath coming in short gasps. He glanced back. They were right behind him, and closing fast. *Wake up, wake up, wake up.* But he couldn't.

He stopped at the water's edge. Looking out, all he saw was a wall of darkness. Then he saw it—out in the ocean, a blazing ship. Orange flames enveloped the entire ship but yet, as improbable as it seemed, he saw robust sails, the ornate bow and stern and a flag rippling in the wind defying the crimson color of fire. The flag was black with a clearly visible skull and cross-bones, a pirate ship.

He didn't know why, but he suddenly turned into the ocean and waded out into the water.

The monsters stopped at the shoreline, growling threateningly, but would not enter.

Heart thumping uncontrollably, he waded waist-deep, glanced behind at the snarling predators momentarily and eyeballed the ship. Something else caught his eye. There were pirates aboard, walking around, fully costumed, a few even waving him aboard.

He waded deeper into the water.

He felt it before he heard it. Lightning fast, a pig-headed monster clamped its enlarged fangs into the back of his neck.

The pain was excruciating.

He pointed the machine gun, squeezed the trigger and multiple rounds smashed through the predator's head, sending him whipping back and splashing into the ocean. But Byron knew it wouldn't be long before the beast resurfaced and renewed its attack with more determination and anger than ever.

So he slung the machine gun over his shoulder and swam for his life, instinctively knowing his salvation lay in reaching and boarding the pirate ship.

He reached the ship, penetrated the surrounding flames without incident, and the flaming pirates extended hands and helped him aboard.

*Out of the frying pan into the fire.*

He coughed water as he lay on deck, surrounded by curious eighteenth-century pirates. He glanced ashore, but the blackness prevented him from seeing the monsters. But, in the distance, he could hear their snarls and the blood-curdling screams of more victims.

What was happening?

A pirate stepped through the circling mass, clad entirely in black.

"This ship has been cursed by the devil," the dark man said. "We need the help of the living to lift the curse."

Byron opened his mouth to speak. But no words would emerge, his throat now constricted with fear.

The dark man unsheathed a large ornate sword, raised it threateningly above his head. "You will help us."

"I can ..."

"Wake up ... wake up ... wake up, Byron?"

He opened his eyes abruptly to the winsome green eyes of Akila staring concernedly at his sweat-soaked face. He shielded it with a forearm instinctively, a disoriented mind slow to register the love of his life. He thought, but only for a split second, his senses had deceived him. That it was the dark pirate about to decapitate him with the lethal blade.

Slowly the horrific images of the nightmare faded and he surveyed the surroundings. He was lying on the hardwood floor, had fallen off the bed during the nightmare. Even the pain of the three-foot fall had not woken him.

He slowly sat up, wincing at a sharp pain in the small of his back.

"I had a nightmare."

"I know. I heard you fall off the bed ... heard you talking in your sleep. But I couldn't wake you. Are you okay?"

"I don't know ... my back's sore. I'll be okay."

"You sure?"

"Yeah." He wasn't.

She helped him up. "I'm going to make breakfast. Why don't you shower? You can tell me all about your nightmare when you're finished."

She kissed him, walked to the bedroom door, stopped and spun around. "If you want to talk about it, that is."

The hot water cascading off his body, Byron couldn't help spinning the dark images around in his head. Two nightmares, less than a week apart. Monsters dying, coming back to life. Sure, he had had nightmares before, hell—most of his story ideas were inspired by nightmares, but he couldn't remember waking with such haunting feelings of dread and premonition.

And the vision—if he could call it that—of a smiling Elias atop a tower, which he knew with a gloomy certainty was the East Point Lighthouse. Riley's comments at the lighthouse—something about his wife coming back. What the hell was he on about?

He didn't know, but he felt certain the vision of a resurrected Elias, East Point Lighthouse, the burning pirate ship and the old caretaker were all mysteriously connected. And, he decided, toweling himself dry and staring in the mirror at his wrung-out reflection, that one way or another he was going to find the answers.

The question was could he handle it?

Over breakfast, he explained the terrifying nightmare to Akila, watching the color drain from her face.

When he was finished, she asked: "Have you heard the legend of the burning phantom ship?"

Byron knew the island was rich with pirate and ghost folklore. But that story had evaded him. "No."

"The legend dates back as early as 1786. Apparently, a pirate ship full of stolen treasure somehow caught fire while sailing just off the coast. It was about to sink, along with all the loot."

They had finished breakfast, bacon, eggs and toast, and Byron sipped coffee as the bright rays of early afternoon sun shone in the kitchen window.

"What happened next?"

"The pirates were worried about their treasure being found." She paused for effect. "So they made a pact with the devil. The devil agreed to hide their treasure so it would never be found. In return, the pirates had to sail forever on the burning ship."

Byron paused, allowing the full weight of the information to settle in his troubled mind. "I saw that ship."

"So have a lot of other people. Some of them swear to it."

"So what do we do now?"

"I don't know but I'm a little worried about Susanne."

After their tour of the lighthouse, they had taken a scenic drive to Poverty Beach, where they had spent the afternoon. They had eaten most of the KFC chicken and salads, enjoyed a swim in the ocean and spent the remainder of the day on a blanket, drinking alcohol and talking. Susanne's mood had begun to brighten mid-way through the day, but toward the end, just as they were packing up to leave, her face had grown somber, maybe the result of one too many road-pops. She had started harping on the strange encounter with Riley and his comment about his dead wife returning. It had been all they could do to prevent her from returning to the lighthouse that evening to investigate what the strange old man was up to.

And they weren't even sure after they had dropped her off that she hadn't decided to return by herself, even though they made her promise not to drive out there alone.

"I don't think she would have gone out there, do you?"

"No, not last night, but it sure sounded like her curiosity was getting the better of her. Who's to say she isn't planning on going there today, for all we know?"

Byron had hoped to spend the day with Akila, and Akila alone. But right now he knew the mental health and safety of their friend was at stake. He wasn't about to turn his back on Susanne in a time of need.

"Why don't you call her?"

"You should have been a mind reader." Akila reached for her cell phone.

Byron stared out at the single maple tree in their backyard as she talked, as if the answer to the strange connections in his head could somehow be found there, or in the tweets of the chickadees.

"You're what?" Akila said after a few minutes of small talk. She mouthed the words to Byron.

Byron's heart sank. Susanne wanted to visit Riley.

# Chapter Eight

Riley looked like a different man when he approached Byron's black pick-up truck and greeted them in front of his house a few hours later. Although it was a weekday, he wore his Sunday best. A neatly-pressed beige suit, white shirt and canary-yellow tie. Even his grizzled face was cleanly shaven, his short gray hair spiked with what looked like gel.

He radiated happiness.

"I'm so glad you could come. Eleanor can't wait to meet you." Riley said.

Except there was something wrong, Byron knew. To confirm his belief, prior to leaving, he had located and reread the newspaper obituary of the deceased Eleanor Fitzgerald. She was dead, all right. There was no question about that. Then how could she be in the house looking forward to meeting them?

And, according to this joyous man standing in front of them, very much alive.

Riley whispered to white faces: "Please don't let her know she died and came back. Not just yet anyway. I want to let her know that gradually."

He led them inside.

As they stepped inside the turn-of-the-century Victorian-style home on five secluded acres, Byron wondered what the hell they were doing there. The voice of reason should have prevailed—they should have talked Susanne out of it. But, in her grief, he also knew she wasn't about to be denied. And, wasn't there some perverted curiosity in his own mind that needed to be satiated? Wasn't this entire fucked up scenario in some way related to his nightmares? He thought so.

Eleanor, her gray hair pulled back in a bouffant-style bun, greeted them with a smile as soon as they entered the kitchen. She wore blue jeans and a stylish long-sleeved black blouse.

The obit put her at eighty-six. Byron thought she could pass for fifty-five.

Riley kissed his wife on the cheek and motioned his guests inside. They stood at the kitchen entrance, wide-eyed, except Susanne, whose wrinkled brow suggested interest and curiosity.

"You look like you've seen a ghost," Eleanor said, approaching and extending her hand. They made introductions, and she asked: "Why the wide eyes? Please come and sit down for tea."

The handshake was as cold as ice.

As they sat down, the women making small talk, Byron tried not to stare at Eleanor's eyes, even though there was something not quite right about them. They were glazed over; vacant with pupils dilated so wide they appeared black.

But her cheery demeanor suggested something else entirely. "I thank God every day that I'm alive."

Riley cast the guests a knowing look. The meaning was clear: keep your mouth shut, until I can straighten this out.

"My memory is usually very good," Eleanor said, "but the thing I can't piece together is how we got in that lighthouse last night. It seems to me I went to sleep and woke up there. I guess that's the thing about growing old though, you never know when the mind is going to start fading out on you. What do you ...?"

She suddenly rolled her eyes around the room, as if identifying it for the first time.

"You were saying?" Susanne said.

The roaming vacant gaze continued.

"More tea, anyone?" Riley asked.

"I think I will," Eleanor said, snapping out of the trance and smiling at the guests.

Byron was getting freaked out. Spending a Sunday afternoon having tea with a dead woman, and pretending it was a perfectly normal thing to do, was a bit much. "Maybe we should be go ..."

"Sure, I'll have another cup of tea, Mr. Fitzgerald," Susanne said.

Akila's eyes darted from Eleanor to Riley in disbelief. What little color she had remaining, was rapidly draining from her features. She gritted her teeth, the only thing she could think of to prevent herself from dashing from the room and screaming in terror at the top of her lungs.

Byron's eyes registered Akila's increasing fear and he nodded. *Yes, baby, I feel the same way. Hang in there.*

She seemed to read his thoughts and calmed somewhat.

"Anyone else?" Riley said, waving the teapot slowly around the room.

Akila and Byron nodded nervously.

As Riley served tea, Eleanor abruptly jumped up from her chair and fumbled in the cutlery drawer. She produced a large butcher knife and brandished it threateningly. The blade glinted as it caught a ray of incoming sunshine.

Riley spun around and stared at her.

She stepped forward, waving it. Byron abruptly stood. "What're you doing with that?"

Susanne and Akila backed toward the door.

She advanced with the knife. With both hands, Byron grabbed an advancing arm and struggled to free the knife. He was surprised how much strength this woman possessed. She backed him into the kitchen counter effortlessly and a life-or-death struggle ensued. *This nutcase is going to kill me.*

Akila stepped forward, grabbing an empty mug and raising it above Eleanor's head.

Susanne inched forward, glancing around the room, looking for the perfect weapon.

Riley leaped up from his chair, blocking Susanne and Akila from moving toward the struggle. "Don't hurt my Eleanor," he said, spreading his arms wide. "She's a good woman."

Byron frantically pushed Eleanor's wrist, his face flushing with the exertion. But the knife slowly descended toward his throat.

"Leave him alone," Akila shouted in a voice giddy with panic.

Eleanor's expression had become zombie-like and the blade inched closer.

"Hey, someone help me here," Byron said.

Riley snapped out of his trance. "Eleanor, put that thing down," he said, moving closer.

In an instant, some vague semblance of her former self appeared. She forcefully pushed Byron's hands away and tossed the knife into the metal sink.

The room was silent as it clanged—a tinny metal-on-metal sound.

Riley eyed the guests apologetically. "She didn't mean that ... I swear."

"Won't you sit down and have some more tea," Eleanor said, smiling. The vacant eyes were the same, but the disposition noticeably calmer.

"I think it's time to go," Byron said, moving to the door. His knees were weak, his voice hoarse with fear.

Akila grabbed Byron's hand as they moved out of the kitchen. Susanne stood frozen to the spot, unable to take her eyes off Eleanor.

Byron grabbed her arm. "Let's go."

Riley tried to stop them, reaching for Susanne's other arm. "She's fine now. She won't hurt you."

"Come on," Byron insisted, yanking her through the front door.

Akila grabbed her other arm and together they marched Susanne across the grass, as fast as possible.

"Come back," Riley stood on the front porch and called after them. "She's fine now."

They stepped into the pick-up truck and Byron rolled the window down as they backed out. "I'd watch that woman of yours. Whatever happened to her ... she isn't the same anymore. If I was you, I'd be concerned for my health."

"You won't say anything?"

"I don't know."

"What do you mean, you don't know?" Akila said as they sped out of the gravel driveway, creating a billowing cloud of dust. "This isn't some horror story ... where we just do nothing and see what happens. That fucking woman came back from the dead. She tried to kill you. And she's going to kill someone."

"Calm down, please. I didn't know what to say at the time."

From the backseat, Susanne craned her neck, staring behind as the property disappeared. "Elias wouldn't do that."

"Do what?" Akila asked.

"He wouldn't kill someone."

# Chapter Nine

*I know he wouldn't kill someone. Not Elias. Not my sweet Elias.* But Susanne knew on some rational level that her decisions were being motivated by guilt. Guilt because the night before Elias had died, although she hadn't told anyone, they had had a little tiff. It wasn't anything big, really, but it was enough to plant seeds of guilt that were now festering into thick weeds that needed to be tended.

They had argued about the wedding. Elias, who had disowned his family over a business deal gone sour, wanted to elope. Susanne, on the other hand, wanted a grandiose wedding with lots of family and friends invited. They had reached a crossroads. Elias was not prepared to make amends with his family for the sake of a wedding.

But, Susanne had insisted that he need not do so. What she wanted was a wedding with her family, their mutual friends.

But Elias, probably unwisely, had been stubborn about it. He had fallen short of insisting they elope, without actually saying it.

And, just before he had left, Susanne had blurted out something she deeply regretted: "Maybe we need to reconsider the whole wedding."

His face had reddened and he left in a huff, closing the door forcefully, almost slamming it.

When he was gone, Susanne had twirled the whole scenario around in her mind, finally deciding on a compromise she thought would work; have a smaller wedding, not quite the big celebration she had in mind, and after a small reception they could honeymoon in Costa Rica for two weeks. She had even spotted some good deals on the internet. She was sure he would agree and was excitedly awaiting his arrival when the phone call arrived—her soul-mate had died in a fiery inferno.

It was the second nail in her emotional coffin. Not quite two years ago, she had been engaged to another man, Francis Stokely. On the night after he had proposed, they had had a little tiff—about exactly the same issue. The only difference—Francis was close to his parents. But he had wanted a small wedding, she a large celebration.

Two hours after he left in a huff, she had received a phone call from Detective Clay Redmond, informing her Francis had failed to navigate a highway corner properly, careened into a ditch and wrapped his sports car around a telephone pole; dead on impact, mangled beyond recognition. No alcohol had been involved, but Redmond said it appeared excessive speed was a factor.

She took another sip of red wine and glanced at the wall calendar. *Oh no.* Saturday, August 18$^{th}$. No wonder she was indulging. It was two years to the day that Francis had met a tragic and untimely death. An anniversary. An anniversary of death.

Now Elias was dead.

But the seeds of the powerful and useless emotion called guilt were taking hold. Motivated by this all-consuming guilt, her mind sought answers. She wanted Elias back. Riley had his wife back, after all. Maybe Eleanor wasn't quite the same, but Elias would never kill anybody. He was a big teddy bear.

She stared at the phone on the kitchen table and contemplated for the eleventh time calling Riley. He would help her bring Elias back so she could make it all better. Apologize for her stubbornness and tell Elias they could have any kind of wedding he wanted as long as they were together and happy.

She wiped away a fresh tear, took another sip of wine and picked up the phone. The guilt. So powerful. So useless.

*That's ridiculous. You're playing with fire, girl. Put that phone down.* But this time the voice of reason did not prevail. The unkempt weeds of guilt had taken over. It didn't help that she was a little buzzed on wine.

She dialed Riley.

He picked up on the second ring. "Hello."

There was a split second when she thought about hanging up, forgetting the whole thing. But that thought, like the fleeting memory of a long-forgotten nightmare, vanished into thin air as quickly as it had materialized.

Susanne had no idea how much she would regret that call.

# Chapter Ten

*I should call. I really should. It's been a few days. She said she wanted some time alone, but I should call.* Akila sat at the kitchen table sipping a caffeinated tea about nine in the evening worrying about a conundrum that on any other day would have been simple to solve. Pick up the phone, check in and see how Susanne's doing. She supposed the only thing that complicated it was what Susanne had said to her yesterday when they talked: "I would like to take a few days to sort this out in my head. Alone."

So she had honored her friend's privacy request. Elias's funeral was in a few days anyway, so it wouldn't be long before she would have an opportunity to comfort Susanne.

But still something nagged at her. She stared at the phone. *Should I call?* She picked up the phone, was about to dial, then replaced it on the table, glancing out the window at the ominous moon and stars dotting the sky—a curtain of black punctuated by small glittering white lights.

She decided not to call. And there was something else.

Death.

Akila understood it more than she cared to. Her relationship with it was ... well, not quite intimate, but close. A strange coincidence. Almost two years to the day, her parents, who had lived in Boston, were the unfortunate victims of a home invasion gone wrong. Her father had tried to play hero when two armed and masked men stormed into the modest suburban home, held them at gunpoint and demanded money.

Her mother had sat nervously on the couch, while her father overheard the commotion. He had grabbed a handgun from a kitchen drawer, entered the living room and aimed it at the attackers. It was the last living thing he ever did. For his trouble, he received two gunshots to the head. One of the men shot her mother three times in the chest.

They disappeared with the money, one limping from a gunshot wound to the leg, the result of her father's attempt at heroism.

It was little consolation to Akila that both men were now behind bars. That couldn't bring back her parents.

After the tragedy, it had been months before she could talk to people, preferring instead to be alone with her thoughts and misery. After almost a year of solitude and grief, she finally came to grips with the fact that death was one of the very few certainties of life.

Slowly she began to view her life through a glass half full. Life is short, so make the most of it. She had to admit her recent suspense novel, *Rise from Darkness*, had helped her through the grieving process. Writing the novel, exploring the violent maelstrom of emotions that envelop your mind when loved ones are snatched away so unexpectedly and violently, had been liberating and therapeutic. Creation of the book, which was garnering positive reviews and starting to climb the Amazon sales charts, had saved her from getting sucked into a dark abyss of misery, despair and depression—one that could have easily led to a cynicism and contempt for humans and their capacity for random and unprovoked acts of violence and murder.

That's why she didn't want to bother Susanne. She wanted her to come to grips with things on her own terms, in her own time, knowing that if she was needed she would be summoned. And she would make a point of being there for Susanne.

But still Susanne's expression when she had met Eleanor worried Akila. She could almost hear the wheels turning in Susanne's head. She wanted Elias back and she had been thinking of a way to do that.

And Akila knew, although she had tactfully not mentioned it, today marked the anniversary of Francis's death. Susanne was also wrestling with some debilitating emotions.

She absently stared at the calendar and grimaced. Tomorrow marked the two-year anniversary of her parents' death.

What a coincidence of carnage.

And with that thought, came the sudden realization that she needed to call the police. What had they been thinking? There was a woman walking around whose obituary was plastered all over the local papers.

Were they supposed to sit idly by while Eleanor walked around, zombie-like, occasionally satisfying an urge to attack people with a butcher knife? She had tried to kill Byron. What about Riley? How long before he ended up sliced and diced?

She didn't know. But she knew with an unsettling certainty that call *had* to be made.

She picked up the phone as Byron entered. As is the case with the often twisted psyche of a writer, he had retreated into his writer's roost a few hours ago, eager to document some of the crazy events of late and incorporate them into the latest work, *Resurrected Souls*.

He had the bleary-eyed, faraway expression of a writer who has immersed himself completely in the minds of his characters. So much for taking a break from writing.

Akila had set the phone down. "Did you find your muse?"

"My muse found me," Byron said, pouring some coffee. It's what kept him going during those long writing stints. He had been at it for five hours.

"How many words?"

"I don't count anymore. I used to get preoccupied with it, but now I try and concern myself with the story. Roughly two thousand I think. Not sure."

Her eyes narrowed. "Do you realize you're immersing yourself in another book, possibly at Susanne's peril?"

Byron sipped his coffee and thought. *What am I doing anyway? She's right. Is that all I concern myself with is a story? What about Susanne? What about my relationship? I was supposed to take some time off, tighten the bond, but I'm right back at it, like a recovering alcoholic and his booze. I'm addicted to writing.*

It was one of his flaws. When things got stressful, he would retreat to the familiar comfort of his vivid imagination, lose himself in the lives of characters, immersing into an invented world—living life vicariously through his creations. But, there was some strange shit going on right now that he hadn't invented. Reality, he supposed, was sometimes stranger than fiction—even more interesting.

Why couldn't he face reality at times? Was it his background? His father certainly hadn't been a good role model, boozing, womanizing, not paying attention to the three children—one girl and two boys. His mother did the best she could, but there was always an undercurrent of tension in the household. She wasn't happy with his father but stayed with him for thirty years, only divorcing after the last son had left to forge his own independence in a crazy, mixed-up world. It was a mark of that generation. Keep the family together. Was it the right choice? Byron didn't think so, but he didn't blame his mother anymore. There was no point to it. She did the best she could in the generation she grew up in.

But it had led to Byron acting out as a young teenager, getting into all kinds of trouble with the law. Luckily, it was all juvenile stuff, break and enter, a few grocery store thefts, a possession of marijuana charge, driving with stolen license plates, no registration and no insurance.

He hung out with some shady characters.

At nineteen, he had seen the light and moved from Toronto, Ontario, to Vancouver, BC. His high school guidance counselor had probably saved his life, pulling him aside one day, while leaving an English class stoned on pot, and saying, "When you graduate, you shouldn't stay in Toronto. If you do, you'll end up in jail."

He hadn't given the advice much thought at the time, was too much of a rebel, but soon after he graduated, the counselor's words had resonated with an insight he couldn't ignore. So, he had put all the bad memories behind, moved to Vancouver and managed to forge a reasonably happy and successful existence. He was close with his mother, didn't talk to his father, and hardly spoke to his brother or sister. Eventually he realized his past didn't matter and he was the shepherd of his own soul. If he wanted to be happy, he had to forge that happiness through hard work and the right decisions, including associations with morally upright people.

Perhaps a little too judgmental, he didn't have a lot of close friends, a mere handful spread across the country. He might not have 500 Facebook friends, didn't even own an account, but he knew the friends he did have would give him the shirt off their backs. They were loyal to a fault.

His mind drifted back to Susanne. She was one of his good friends. Her loyalty was impenetrable. *What about my loyalty?*

His gaze slowly lifted from the cup of java and met Akila's sad eyes. She had been staring at him, knowing he was lost in the inner recesses of a troubled mind. She knew him well. "Why don't we call her?" he asked.

"I've been agonizing over that for the last few hours. She wanted private time."

"What do you want to do?"

"I think we should call the police."

Byron had already churned this scenario around in his mind previously. He knew she was right. "Okay."

Akila picked up the phone and called Detective Redmond. She explained things, finishing with: "I know you will find this hard to believe ... but I think we've got a psychotic dead woman with a propensity for violence on the loose."

Redmond seemed unsurprised by the news. He promised to visit Riley tomorrow to see what was going on.

For now, she had left her concerns about Susanne out of the equation. When she was finished, she hung up. She turned to Byron. "He might want to talk to us tomorrow."

Byron nodded, searching her eyes. Her furrowed brow suggested a pain that went beyond the death of Elias or her concern for Susanne, but he couldn't be sure.

*Am I forgetting something?*

# Chapter Eleven

*Am I forgetting something?* Susanne double-checked a small backpack before starting the green SUV: two flashlights, bottled water, wine, screwdrivers, hammer, crowbar and corkscrew. Satisfied, she fired it up, shoulder-checked and cautiously pulled out into the night.

She knew Riley would have the dolly, would know how to access the funeral home and get the coffin to the lighthouse and, most importantly, resurrect Elias.

She had surrendered to guilt and told Riley in no uncertain terms, "I want Elias back."

He was reluctant at first, perhaps because Eleanor had threatened them with a butcher knife. That was a pretty damned good reason to be cautious about resurrecting anyone else. But, after Susanne had broken down in tears on the phone, the numbing effects of the wine bubbling her emotions to the surface, Riley had finally acquiesced.

They had hatched a plan. He would meet her at the funeral home, help her to steal the coffin containing Elias and together they would bring him to East Point Lighthouse or, as Riley called it, Resurrection Point. He had confided in her that the secret to immortality had everything to do with the lighthouse.

Riley had a friend, Samuel Longhorn, who would help. But the only thing that nagged at Susanne was when she had asked what the pirate wanted in return for the resurrection. Riley had paused momentarily and said: "I don't know. I haven't gotten that far yet."

Well, it was too late now. She pulled down the dark alley and parked in the small parking lot behind the funeral home. *Oh shit. Wire cutters.* She had forgotten to bring the wire cutters. The buzz of the wine, her grief, the all-consuming guilt clogging her mind like a plugged artery.

She exited the vehicle with the small knapsack. Like clockwork, Riley pulled in beside her.

"Did you bring wire cutters?" she asked as he exited.

He nodded. "Are you sure you want to go through with this?"

Susanne thought about it for a moment. Then she nodded. "Okay, let's get going."

He pulled the dolly out, slung a duffle bag over his shoulder and proceeded to the rear door.

Susanne followed, glancing around nervously. Except for the intermittent roop, roop, roop of a barking dog, the night was quiet and still, the sky clear, the full moon luminously proclaiming its ominous presence.

Riley snipped some wires at the door, turned around and said: "Crowbar please," as calmly and authoritatively as a heart surgeon would ask a nurse for scalpel.

She handed over the crowbar. He reefed on the inside crack of the steel door. It protested with a squeak but then snapped open with a metallic clang.

They paused, glancing around to see if anyone had heard.

The night was quiet. Even the yapping dog had shut its mouth.

"Flashlight."

Susanne produced two flashlights and handed one to Riley. They quickly entered and stealthily moved down the dark hall.

"Do you know where he is?" Riley said.

"Yeah." There had been a recent viewing of the coffin, although it had been a closed-casket affair. Susanne dreaded to think how Elias looked now after being torched extra crispy in a blazing inferno. She hoped Samuel could restore his handsomeness.

He stepped aside. "You lead, then."

She led the way down a few hallways and into a drearily dark room where a lonely coffin stood.

Riley stopped, scratching his head in confusion.

"What's wrong?"

"That's a heavy coffin. I'm not sure we can get it on the dolly."

Susanne had a grisly image of opening up the coffin to the remains of Elias's body spilling out onto the floor in a pile of blood, guts and disconnected bones. She shuddered. "Is there any other way?"

He scratched his head. "Wait a minute. Wait here." He disappeared and, after what appeared to be an agonizingly long time, reappeared with a wheel-equipped stretcher, specifically designed for efficient transport of coffins.

"Help me slide this over here." Riley positioned the stretcher alongside the coffin and smiled a toothy grin that seemed strangely psychotic in the faint glow of LED flashlight beams.

They slid the coffin onto the stretcher and abruptly stopped and fell silent, listening to the slow creaking sound of a door swinging open.

They froze.

Susanne felt her heartbeat thudding violently in her chest, the mild wine buzz giving way to an adrenaline-induced lucidity and heightening of senses.

Riley held an index finger to his mouth and they locked wide eyes and listened.

Silence.

"It's nothing," he whispered.

Susanne was having second thoughts. "Aren't you going to check it out?"

"What difference will it make? If it's the cops, we're busted."

She supposed he was right. With great effort, they slid the coffin onto the stretcher, wheeled it down the winding hallway and into the moonlit parking lot.

The retractable wheels lined up perfectly with the truck. In a few minutes, Elias, coffin and stretcher, securely tied in place, were barreling down the highway.

Susanne followed nervously, close behind. *What the fuck am I thinking?*

But she knew it was too late to back out now. For better or worse, she was going to resurrect Elias and apologize. Then she would plan a wedding exactly the way he wanted it. And they would live happily ever after.

*I'm sure of it.*

# Chapter Twelve

"Are you sure of it ... I mean sure of this," Riley said.

Susanne nodded resolutely. Any lingering doubts had evaporated.

Riley had backed the pick-up flush with the lighthouse door, jury-rigged a piece of plywood on the open tailgate and, with great effort, they had slid the coffin down the plywood. It had skidded to a landing on the floor inside the lighthouse.

They closed the door and stood over the coffin.

Susanne was too afraid to open it.

"I hope he's here," Riley said, looking around.

"Who?"

"Samuel Longhorn. Remember?"

"Oh, yeah. What do we do now?"

"I call him."

"He comes at your bidding?"

"He did last time." He took a few paces into the dark room. "Samuel ... Are you here? I have another one for you."

Silence.

"What does he want in return?" asked Susanne.

"I told you ... I don't know yet. Why don't you ask him? Samuel ... there's a favor I need."

They waited in silence for a few minutes but nothing happened. The only sound was the gentle lapping of the waves on the sandy shoreline below the fifty-foot high red cliffs.

"Are you sure this is going to work?"

"No ... But it worked for Eleanor."

"How is she?"

"Much better than before. I think that ... ah, attack was just kind of an adjustment or something. She seems much more herself lately."

"That's go ..."

A slow and steady whistling sound from above interrupted the sentence. It grew louder, and a large gray-white mist descended upon them, swaying side-to-side like a listlessly floating feather.

At the sight of the eerie vision, Susanne's nerves got the better of her, not to mention the pain in her head from the ear-splitting sound. Riley seemed oblivious. She raced out the door, arrived at her SUV, opened the door, fished around for the bottle of wine and corkscrew and opened the bottle. The whistling sound was deafening, the whole operation, if you could call it that, overwhelming. She wasn't sure of much right now. Just that she needed some liquid confidence to get through this. With an unsteady hand, she tilted the bottle to her mouth and took a long pull. Draining about five mouthfuls, she stopped and listened.

The whistling had stopped. The pain in her head slowly subsided. Her heart rate returned to normal—as normal as it could be under the circumstances.

Bottle in one hand, flashlight in the other, she reentered the lighthouse.

The coffin was open. And empty. Riley had disappeared.

She heard a faint scraping sound echoing from the top of the lighthouse and slowly ascended the spiral staircase. She reached the landing one floor below the lantern room, stopped and heard the clunking of footsteps.

The black boots and blue coveralls of Riley were visible, climbing down the stairs. He turned to her, smiling. Then she saw it.

A pair of flip-flop style sandals, the torn cuffs of a pair of faded Levis—the casual attire of Elias Masters. The rest of his body, his face emerged. His head spun around—much too fast—and smiled, the infectious smile that never failed to brighten a room.

He had been resurrected. Other than a vacant, faraway look in his eyes, he was none the worse for wear. His mangled corpse had been miraculously restored to its original splendor.

"Hi honey ... I'm home."

Her mouth dropped and eyes lit up. Everything was going to be all right after all.

# Chapter Thirteen

"It's not fucking all right," Detective Clay Redmond snapped.

"I didn't mean it's all right ... I meant all right. As in, I'll do it." Constable Ronald McCafferty cowered from his superior's caustic tone.

"Well, do it then. Get the fuck out of here."

McCafferty paused, but quickly thought twice about opening his mouth. He knew the detective's moods by now, knew if he said anything else it would be followed by a vitriolic verbal onslaught. He spun around and left the office, being careful to gently close the door. He had been reamed out in the past for slamming it and didn't want to suffer round two of the wrath of Redmond.

It might well be a knock-out punch.

Redmond, a seasoned detective, wasn't in a particularly good mood that morning. He was borderline furious. The morning hadn't started off well; first a call from a female manager at East Point Lighthouse, saying in frightened and serious tones that last night someone had started a bonfire beside the tower and roasted a wooden picnic table. Anabelle Richter had her theories, blaming the "random act of violence" on drunk and delinquent teenagers partying. But she had no proof, not even a debris mound of beer can empties to support her claim.

Redmond had just been hanging up the phone when another call had come in—this one from the local funeral home owner. Someone had broken in last night and stolen the body and coffin of the late Elias Masters.

If that wasn't enough, Akila had only yesterday said that the late wife of Riley Fitzgerald had been resurrected from the dead and that she and Byron had recently enjoyed the pleasure of her company over a nice hot cup of tea—albeit followed by a spontaneous and unprovoked murder attempt with a butcher knife.

His day's itinerary already included a visit to Riley's house—and he had to swing out to the lighthouse afterward and still try and squeeze in a one-on-one with Akila.

Now this goddamned call about the missing coffin and corpse. He couldn't be in three places at once. So, he had ordered McCafferty to deal with it. But the newbie had hesitated, as if there was a lot to think about, and then came back with that stupid comment. That's when the veins in Redmond's neck had bulged, the color of his cheeks flushing to an almost perfect match with his shortly-cropped red hair.

He scrubbed the two-day growth on his chin and pondered the rapidly escalating and disturbing events. Riley's wife was back? Riley worked as a caretaker at East Point Lighthouse. Elias' body had disappeared from the funeral home a day before the funeral. Susanne Watterton, Elias's fiancé, had been with Akila and Byron when they visited Riley and his dead—or apparently very much alive—wife. The recent fire at the lighthouse. It wasn't rocket science to connect the dots.

Riley and the lighthouse somehow played a part in the resurrection of Eleanor—if she was indeed alive. Riley and Susanne were somehow connected to the disappearance of Elias. What was burned at the lighthouse besides the picnic table? A coffin? The body of Elias?

Why now? Two days before he was supposed to take a well-deserved vacation to Punta Cana in the Dominican Republic. *Fuck, the timing sucks.*

He grimaced, picked up some files and left the office. The bright sunny day did little to lift his spirits. But he knew one thing that would—a cold beer and some attractive female company.

In the police station parking lot, he started his black unmarked Crown Vic. The extra-curricular stuff would have to wait, he knew. Once on a case, like a hungry lion stealthily stalking an unsuspecting gazelle in the wild, he stayed close to his prey.

He lit a cigar, quietly cursed the shitty timing of the horrible events, and floored it, the screeching of tires and a cloud of blue smoke trailing his exit.

An elderly lady limping down the street with a cane shot an admonishing glare and he bit his tongue so he wouldn't bend to a knee-jerk reaction and flip the bird out the open window.

Leaving Charlottetown, he pondered. Go to Riley's first or the lighthouse? Wait a minute. Riley would be working at the lighthouse today. Shit. With all the hard-boiled cases he had been working lately, the old mental muscle wasn't firing on all cylinders. Brain drain. He needed a vacation. Badly. But what about Eleanor? She would be at home, or at least should be at home if what Akila said was true.

He decided to visit the lighthouse first, in case Riley decided to lie about Eleanor and discourage a visit to his home. Besides, he was curious to find out what had been burned at the bonfire last night. Redmond thought he knew, but he wanted it confirmed.

Forty-five minutes later, he arrived. He questioned Anabelle, the gift shop manager. She told him it was Riley's day off. He went outside and inspected the ashy remains of the bonfire. It was still smoldering. He bent down to inspect the ashes and partial remains of a picnic table—evidently used as kindling to burn something much larger. He kicked the ashes with his black boots and something skidded across the charred circle of dirt. He picked it up and examined it. A solid brass handle—for a coffin. With a gloved hand, he dropped it into a plastic evidence bag.

And there was something else. The recent rains had softened the grass around the small park and he detected large tire ruts a few feet from the lighthouse entrance. Someone had driven up to the front door. For what? To pick something up. Or drop something off? Something heavy. The coffin?

He scratched his stubble and examined the rest of the park for about another half hour. Finding nothing, he left.

Ten minutes later, he arrived at Riley's secluded acreage.

The old man was in the garage welding as he arrived. The truck was parked beside the garage. Redmond exited the Crown Vic and glanced at the truck tires—caked with mud and grass.

Riley stepped out into the hot afternoon sun, wiped a sweaty brow and greeted the detective with a warm smile. Redmond was well known in these parts, particularly for his ability to hunt down killers. If he wasn't able to prove anything within the confines of the law, he'd been known to break the law. A few of the killers had disappeared without a trace. While locals suspected he operated outside the law (if the wheels of justice were not turning in his favor) they couldn't prove anything.

Besides, they didn't care how he did it. As long as he cleansed the island of scumbags, solidified and reinforced the squeaky-clean and laid-back tourist image. Locals considered Redmond a hero. He had so much public support he was practically beyond reproach by the captain of the force. He had the power of the people watching his back.

Now he exited the car, wincing slightly as a pain shot up his lower back. He was in his late forties, but sometimes the back felt like that of an eighty-five-year-old—goddamned sciatica.

Riley examined his hand as the detective approached.

"I'd shake your hand, Clay, but this one's greasy as hell."

"No problem, Riley." He glanced inside the two-car garage at the old convertible. There was some fresh sheet metal that had just been tack-welded onto a left rear quarter panel. A cloud of pale blue smoke hung in the air. "You fixing the old beast up?"

He smiled. "Yeah. Finally decided to get to it."

Redmond occasionally shared coffee and conversation with Riley. In their ten-year relationship, he had never known Riley to be anything other than honest, loyal, trustworthy and friendly. His reputation was solid. He decided to take the good cop approach. If Riley was hiding something, he didn't want to anger the man, even though Riley was known to be as gentle as a teddy bear.

"Day off today, Riley?"

"Yeah."

"Did you hear about the fire at the lighthouse last night?"

Riley glanced at his grease-stained hands. "I did—terrible thing what these kids will do."

"Is that who you think it was? Kids?"

"Who else?"

"I suppose. You weren't out last night?"

"Stayed in watching television. You know ... things haven't been the same for me since Eleanor passed."

"She passed onto a better place." Redmond wasn't a religious man but he didn't know what else to say.

"What's this all about anyway?"

"Well ... I can't name my sources, but it seems someone thinks your wife is alive."

"That's ridiculous." After a moment's pause: "I had Akila, Byron and Susanne here the other day ... and I talked about how great it would be if Eleanor was back ... but, Clay, come on. We both know someone can't be resurrected from the dead." Riley was sure Susanne wouldn't breathe a word about Eleanor, especially since she now had her hubby back, but he wasn't sure about Akila and Byron. It was probably them. How could he have been so stupid?

"Listen, people tell me things. I have to check them out. That's my job. You sure you didn't go anywhere last night?"

"Stayed home."

"Your tires look a little muddy, like you've been out not too long ago."

"Uhh ... I was in the back field last night cleaning out some stumps."

Redmond glanced around the acreage and saw no evidence of tire tracks. "Did you hear what happened at Montgomery Funeral Home last night?"

Riley returned his glance to his sweaty palms. He shook his head.

"Someone broke in and stole the corpse and coffin of Elias Masters?"

"Susanne's fiancé?"

"How did you know that?"

"I read the papers, Clay. And she was just out here the other day."

The detective nodded. He was certain of it now: Riley was as guilty as a three dollar bill.

But he wasn't going to call the man's bluff. Not yet anyway. If he wanted to learn what Riley was hiding, it would be more effective to feign ignorance for a while. He thought about asking the man to inspect his home, but changed his mind. Riley had probably learned from the lighthouse gift store cashier the detective was on his way out. He was expecting the visit. No. Eleanor, if she had indeed been resurrected from the dead, was in a safe hiding place. He wouldn't be able to find her if he tried.

And without Riley's permission, he needed a search warrant. And that wasn't something that would happen overnight. Besides, what was he guilty of? Stealing a corpse and a coffin? Bringing back his wife from the dead? What was the charge for that anyway?

But night surveillance would be in order; maybe a job for eager-to-impress rookie Ronald McCafferty.

Right now, Redmond had other more pressing concerns on his mind. He wanted to visit the funeral home. But first he wanted to talk to Susanne, Akila and Byron in that order.

He knew if Elias was anywhere, he would be with Susanne—dead or undead.

They made some small talk about the weather, how much Redmond was looking forward to his vacation, before Redmond said goodbye.

Riley stood watching the detective return to the Crown Vic.

Redmond opened the car door. He paused for a second before climbing in, glancing back at Riley. "If you find out anything about the bonfire, you let me know. I don't take too kindly to people destroying important tourist attractions."

Riley's brow furrowed. "You bet, Clay. I'll be sure to do that."

# Chapter Fourteen

"You sure you want to do that?" Susanne asked.

"Of course I'm sure," Elias said. "Get in."

Susanne hesitantly regarded her fiancé from the dock near Point Pleasant. He wanted to go on an evening speed boat tour around Murray Islands—specifically Gordon's Island, part of a small cluster of islands that dotted the southeastern coast. It seemed like he had a purpose, although he wouldn't say as much.

Maybe the purpose was to escape Detective Redmond's interrogation?

Earlier in the day, as the detective had pulled up to their house, they had backed out of the rear garage, rolled down the alley and disappeared. A few hours later, they had parked Susanne's SUV a few blocks away and stealthily returned home. The phone rang five, maybe six times but Susanne had not answered.

What was she supposed to say? I've just resurrected Elias from the dead and we want some time alone. Could you call back later please? Besides, she knew Redmond wanted to question her and, knowing full well his stellar reputation on PEI, she didn't think she could fool a sharp-witted and sagacious man like him. Not until she had a chance to sort herself out and figure out a plausible explanation. And what sort of plausible explanation could she invent to explain a resurrected and almost normal Elias Masters?

Normal. No, not quite; almost normal—yes. Arriving home last night, Susanne had been elated to have her man back. They had stayed up a good part of the night making love. And she had enjoyed most of it. But there was a change in him. Subtle at first but as time passed more noticeable and disturbing. His eyes, first of all. At times, she saw the man she loved in those deep blue eyes. But other times, there was a cold and distant stare, along with a faraway, unfocused and eerie blankness in the depths of those dilated pupils.

And there was something else. He would be talking to her one minute and the next he would blank out, his eyes rolling up in his head in an almost introspective manner. And some weird, ineffable transformation would pervade his boyish features and be replaced by something evil and sinister. And, in an instant, it would disappear and be replaced by the Elias of old.

It creeped her out—big time.

From the speed boat gently lolling in the water, he waved her in. "What are you waiting for? Come on."

He extended a hand. She took it and climbed aboard. She was in now—hook, line and sinker. And they hadn't planned on fishing.

He started the engine and they sped away from the shoreline and out to sea.

She had no idea what she was doing. But, to stick around the house also meant answering some tough questions from Redmond, Byron and Akila. And she didn't want to think about that right now.

*Relax*, she told herself. *Everything's going to be okay.*

As Elias navigated the small craft, she got comfortable and tried to enjoy the surrounding beauty: the dark sky, ominously glowing full moon, twinkling stars, the odd beached seal lumbering clumsily into the water and gracefully swimming away as soon as it became one with its element.

She reached into the cooler and extracted a vodka cooler. Vodka was made from potatoes. Potatoes are good for you. A little mind-numbing refreshment certainly wouldn't hurt right now. She twisted the cap off and took a long pull, settling in beside the steering captain, putting an arm around him.

He smiled, the Elias of old.

"Why do you want to go to Gordon's Island anyway?" Susanne asked.

"Have you ever been there?"

"No."

"It's beautiful. A tiny island, but lots of nice forested bits and a nice little beach. We can hang out, have a few drinks and enjoy the peacefulness."

"Probably lots of seals too."

He refocused on the boat's trajectory. "I'll bet."

They approached the cluster of tiny islands and Elias expertly weaved the small craft onward. Susanne returned to the cooler and opened another vodka cooler. Potatoes. Good for you. She removed the cap and took a long drink, the sedating effects of the alcohol starting to take hold. "Do you want one?"

"Not yet," he said.

*When am I going to tell him about our wedding—exactly the way he wants it to be. Not yet, but soon. Maybe when we reach Gordon's Island.*

Something caught Susanne's eye. In the distance, behind one of the islands, a soft orange glow. As they got closer, an eerie fiery image appeared. She rubbed her eyes in disbelief.

What? A flaming ship, its ominous orange glow silhouetting the dark horizon.

Elias slowed the boat to an idle, spun around, smiling knowingly. "There it is."

Susanne's eyes widened in horror. "What are you taking about?" She dropped the vodka cooler and it rolled along the floor, its contents fizzing out.

"Can't you see it?"

"I can see it. But's what's ... what's it supposed to mean?"

Elias, without responding, revved the motor and bee-lined it right for the phantom ship.

Susanne grabbed another vodka cooler. She would need a little more alcohol to deal with what was in store. Of that, she was certain.

Elias pulled up to within thirty feet of the phantom ship, killed the engine and stood up. Their boat bobbed in the choppy waters. He eyed her with that same vacant stare she had seen before, but this time there was something resolute in the eyes—something that said he was on a mission.

He pointed. "Can you see them?"

She returned her gaze to the ship. It was a large vessel. Little black dots danced in the translucent flames. She looked closer. Those weren't little black dots—they were people.

Susanne felt the color drain from her face. "I think we should go home."

"What for? Let's pull up to that beach over there and watch the show."

She was about to protest, but it was too late. He had already started the boat and was guiding it slowly to a wooden makeshift dock. As they approached, he killed the engine, jumped out and tied the boat off. A few seals, disturbed by the uninvited guests, flopped into the water and disappeared.

Susanne felt the tiny hairs on the back of her neck stick out. A cold chill swept up her spine, finding an unwelcome home in her brain. Brain freeze—and not the kind from drinking a frosty drink too fast.

Elias' expression was dead-pan. "Come on. Let's sit on the beach and enjoy the show." He said it as perfunctorily as if they were preparing to watch a fireworks demonstration. Maybe they were.

"I think we should leave." The tone of Susanne's voice had become panicked, the decibel level ratcheted up a few notches. She wasn't enjoying herself anymore.

"Leave? We just got here." His eyes lost the vacant glaze momentarily and became pleading.

*Is this the Elias I know and love?* She stared at him for a long moment. On a sudden and unexplainable impulse, she grabbed the cooler, took his outstretched hand and he guided her out of the boat, down the dock and onto the beach.

Rigid with tension, she sat beside Elias in the sand, drinking. He drank a vodka cooler also. He put an arm on her shoulder and she shuddered. His skin was as cold as her vodka cooler.

They stared at the luminescent ship floating about a hundred feet from shore, bobbing side to side. A few seals swam around it, occasionally poking their heads up curiously before disappearing back into the misty, black ocean water.

Some of the dark silhouetted pirates had gathered at the bow and eerily stared at them from the vessel, tiny red dots for eyes glowing amidst the orange flame engulfing the ship.

Susanne took a long pull on the cooler. She had heard about the phantom ship, but had considered it island folklore, fiction and nothing more. But the presence in front of her told a different story. It had a power that seemed to draw her in, darken her thoughts like massive black thunder clouds threatening to erupt at any second and wreak a devastating swath of destruction through her psyche.

She fought to control her emotions. Swallowed hard at the lump ascending in her throat, trying to force it back into the pit of her stomach lest it spew forth as an uncontrollable wave of panic.

Some part of Elias sensed her nervousness. He removed his transfixed gaze from the fiery ship and searched her eyes. Like a concerned parent reassuring a distressed daughter after she has skinned her knee, he said: "Don't worry, honey. Everything is going to be all right. You're going to be okay. Soon we can really be together."

"What do you mea ..."

A metallic swoosh interrupted Susanne. She spun around and saw it. Pirate Captain Samuel Longhorn had unsheathed a large sword and stood behind her, the silvery metal of the blade glistening orange from the fiery reflection of the ship.

The dark, shadowy figure raised the sword high above his head, eyes glowing blood-red, a menacing smile creeping across obscure features. "I'm glad you could come, Susanne. I hope you enjoy your resurrected life."

Her eyes widened as she felt Elias's grip tighten on her arm. *What's he doing? Holding me in place while this nutcase decapitates me?*

She reacted instinctively and smashed Elias in the head with the vodka cooler bottle. The glass shattered and a cut instantly opened up on his forehead, snaking tiny rivulets of blood into his eyes and across his nose. His grip loosened, eyes becoming dazed.

As the sword came down in an arc, one that would have sliced through her neck, she rolled quickly and it cut into the sand hard.

She sprinted toward the forest before she knew what was even happening.

"Susanne," Elias said in a dazed tone. "Come back!"

She didn't look back, but heard footsteps clapping on the water-saturated sand, growing louder. She hit the tree line, found a small trail and kept running, breaths coming in short, panicked gasps.

She tripped over a fallen tree, landed face-first in the dirt before the momentum of the fall shot her somersaulting forward. She rolled twice before landing outstretched on her back. She tasted sour blood on her lip and realized she had cut her nose.

Her knee throbbed. She had skinned it on a rock, slashing it open during the somersaults. She rubbed it for a second, winced, jumped up and continued running, the thudding of footsteps now echoing fainter. She was putting distance between them.

She didn't know if Elias had joined the hunt, didn't care.

The singular need to survive pushed her forward.

Rounding a bend in the trail, she saw a large outcrop of rocks jutting out at odd angles against the backdrop of the shimmering moon. She stopped and studied the dark shapes.

In a macabre way, it resembled the face of some horned demon, a large round hole at the bottom appearing like a mouth agape in a shriek of rage.

*What choice do I have?*

Snapping branches, pulling at a tangled web of forest growth, she proceeded toward the black, ominously gaping mouth.

She finally got clear of the thick growth, climbed some large boulders and stood in front of the black abyss. It was a cave—a four-foot diameter opening.

She ducked her head and stepped in blindly, arms outstretched, rocky cave walls guiding her further inside.

When she thought she was far enough in, she felt her way to a large boulder and sat down, taking deep breaths, struggling to control her breathing for fear of being detected.

She listened.

They were there all right, the echoing thud of approaching footsteps nearing the cave.

She bit her lip to prevent an escaping scream that seemed to have a mind of its own. She tasted more blood trickling inside her mouth.

She listened.

Silence.

After a moment, more footsteps. But wait. The sound of the footsteps grew fainter. They were leaving. She had escaped.

For now.

She waited, shivering in silence for another two minutes. Finally, she removed her hand from her mouth. In her fear, she wasn't even aware she had covered her mouth.

She put her hand down, feeling for the support of the rocky floor and touched something soft.

A hissing sound erupted and she screamed—a short, panicked burst.

Yellow eyes of a raccoon regarded her momentarily before slowly lumbering further into the blackness enveloping the cave. It was his home, after all. She was an unwelcome guest who had disrupted his sleep.

She fought again to control her breathing, wondering if the predators had heard her.

Robbie the Raccoon was the least of her concerns right now.

As her heart rate slowly decreased, she realized with little satisfaction a blanket of quiet had enveloped the night. Random thoughts twirled in her mind. She felt in her jeans pocket. Shit. The cell phone. She had left it on the boat.

The full weight of what she had done slowly began to settle in. She realized she had made a terrible mistake by tampering with the laws of nature, aiding and abetting Elias's resurrection.

*How stupid can you be girl? Actions fuelled by guilt over Francis, guilt over a stupid little tiff with Elias. He's dead. That's not him anymore you crazy mixed-up woman. Haven't you heard the saying, don't flog a dead horse? Or what about, let dead dogs lie? Or, better still, let dead dogs DIE!*

# Chapter Fifteen

"To die for ... this view is absolutely to die for," Riley told his resurrected wife a few minutes later as they chugged toward Murray Islands in a small fishing vessel.

He wasn't far off. The moon and stars shimmering overhead bathed the black ocean waters in a silvery reflective light. Twinkling yellow lights of seashore homes danced across the distant waters. And, other than the small wake the boat created as it glided along, the ocean was calm.

Dead calm.

Riley was at the helm steering, watching the GPS navigation system, monitoring depth and staring ahead at the tiny dark islands growing larger. His wife sat beside him on a barstool.

Eleanor looked at him, smiling reassuringly but said nothing; eyes vacant and unfocused ever since they left the house earlier that evening, narrowly escaping another visit by Detective Redmond, who was growing increasingly more aware.

Riley kept trying to tell himself that everything was going to be okay, and the mickey of Lamb's Navy Rum had gone some way to reaffirming that sentiment. Sure, there was a nagging feeling of anxiety clawing through his mind, but the alcohol had pushed it deep into a locked drawer in a faraway compartment.

He removed the metal flask from his coveralls, took a pull and handed it to Eleanor. She was a teetotaler at the best and worst of times, so he doubted she would indulge. But, it was only polite to ask.

She stared at the flask. Her brow furrowed for a second before she grabbed it, took a couple of gulps, made a face and handed it back to him. "Why not? We need to celebrate our new life together."

Riley took another pull. "I'll drink to that."

They weaved through some of the islands before finally arriving at Gordon's Island, Eleanor pointing the way as if by instinct.

As far as Riley knew, she had never visited Murray Islands. Come to think of it, why, late in the evening, had she suddenly decided that a sojourn in Riley's converted fishing boat was in order?

He scratched his head, puzzling.

"There," she pointed. "Pull up by that dock."

He noticed a speedboat. "Someone else is here."

"Not to worry. It's your friends, Susanne and Elias."

*Friends,* Riley thought, through an enveloping haze. *I only met Suzanne twice and I barely met Elias. How does she know about Elias? Friends? How does she know they're here?*

He slowly docked. They disembarked and walked onto the beach.

Eleanor stared into the dark tree line a short distance from the beach as Riley eyed the footprints, partially washed away at the shoreline but making a distinct and widening pattern to a small trail. He was no detective, but he could tell whoever formed those footprints had sprinted away. *Running. From what?* He felt his old ticker beat faster. "Huh ... where are Susanne and Elias?"

Eleanor sat down on a nearby boulder studying the ocean. "Not to worry, dear. It won't be long now."

*How could she know these things? What's going on here? Why did I come?*

She patted a boulder beside her. "Join me."

Riley sat down, extracted the metal flask, took another long pull, and stared into the dark sky.

"There," Eleanor said. "He's coming."

Riley looked where she was pointing. At first he could see nothing. Then slowly a silvery gray mass materialized out of thin air and descended like an angry tornado. He recognized the image of Samuel Longhorn, draped in a black robe, materialize.

Riley wasn't afraid of Samuel. He had seen him before. In a grief-stricken mission, he thought the man, or apparition, might one day become his friend. He smiled. "Samuel's come for a visit."

Samuel landed on the beach nearby, becoming more distinct. His eyes glowed fiery red. He grinned at the visitors. "You have done an admirable job, Riley. Now we have to complete your mission."

*Complete my mission? What's he talking about? Oh, right. He wants something. He wouldn't bring Eleanor back for nothing.* Riley shuddered. *I hope it's reasonable.*

All he saw out of the corner of his eye was the glint of metal before he realized what had happened. Eleanor, from somewhere in a pocket of her blue jean shirt, extracted a large butcher knife and, with strength he didn't know she possessed, plunged it deep in his chest.

He coughed, gurgled and spewed a mouthful of blood that poured down his chin. He leaped up, gripping the knife handle and staggering on the sand.

"Don't worry dear. We will be together in the resurrected state."

Riley jerked the blade free. Blood squirted from the fatal heart wound. Wide-eyed with horror, he fell on his back like a beached whale. His body twitched for a few seconds before he took a last gurgling gasp and died.

"Good work, my soldier," Samuel said. "Now we need to find Susanne."

# Chapter Sixteen

*What traits do I give Susanne? Do I make her like she is or change the face, give her some characteristics that are different? Guess I don't want to make her too much like Susanne, in case I decide to kill her character and she reads the book. She might not like that.*

Byron stared at the blank white page on the computer screen. He had knocked off about five thousand words in total, averaging around 2,500 a day for the last two days. But this afternoon, he was having trouble starting, as he sometimes did. He generally found if he forced himself to sit down and stare at the blank page long enough eventually the words would come. Then, after writing a few paragraphs, words would often pour out and the story would begin to develop a life of its own.

But not today. He had been staring at a blank page for three hours. He was still staring at it, hadn't written a single word. Oh, other than *Chapter Four*, which didn't count.

It was all he could do to tweak the initial chapters in the hope the muse would appear and guide him through the remainder. But the muse hadn't visited.

So he reviewed, tweaked and thought about the novel's development thus far.

He didn't think the word construction was bad, the character development was coming together, and the writing had a cadence and rhythm that was a signature of his work. He had a rough plot outline, but that was it. But this story was a little different than some of his other fiction. It was pretty closely based on true events. In many ways he was waiting for the story to unfold.

He stared at the blank screen. *Chapter Four. How do I start it?*

Nothing came to mind. He could invent and wait for events to unfold before continuing. But right now, his mind was short of invention. He went into the kitchen, poured himself another cup of coffee, relieved himself in the bathroom and returned to the small office, staring out onto the historic tree-lined residential street. The brightly shining sun did little to inspire his creativity.

He stared at the screen. His mind wandered. Akila had left the house a few hours ago, claiming she was going to drop by Susanne's house. Susanne wasn't answering her phone.

Yesterday, they had provided the detective with all the details involving the strange visit with Riley and Eleanor. They were shocked to learn that Elias's body had been stolen from the funeral home and Redmond suspected Susanne and Riley. So, this morning when they woke up, the plan called for a visit to Susanne's house.

But, some creative inspiration had flooded into Byron's mind as he woke and he wanted to try and document it while it was still fresh. Akila had shown just the slightest annoyance when he had announced he would catch up with her after a few hours of writing. But, he knew her well enough to realize that a slight annoyance visible in her features usually meant a lot more was going on inside her head. They had been together two years. If history had taught him anything, she was mad.

*But wait a minute. Doesn't she have a right to be mad? All the time I've spent on writing, editing, cover design, proofreading, at the expense of my relationship? Fuck, anyone would be mad. Wasn't I supposed to take a break—with her?*

His mind drifted to his other relationships. There was Lisa. After three years, she had declared that he was much too involved in his projects to ever give her the attention she deserved. They hadn't moved in together yet, but had planned on it. One morning, she called out of the blue and said: "This isn't going anywhere. It's over."

Then Leanne. Two years of bliss in Byron's eyes had ended abruptly one day after she had declared: "You have commitment issues, and your projects, especially your writing, give you way more joy than I ever will. Thanks again for your interest and good luck in your future endeavors." The proverbial please fuck off.

Before that, Lina. Four years. A steady erosion of the relationship due to Byron's commitment issues. "You like hanging around with your male friends much better than you like hanging around with me." That relationship had ended ugly. One day while they were enjoying what was supposed to be a relaxing evening in front of the television, a few bottles of wine and some snacks, Lina stood up and said: "You know, you're a fucking asshole. Being with you is like being with a pet rock. I get zero attention and acknowledgement." She stormed into the kitchen and returned with a large knife. She attacked him, swinging the glistening blade wildly. Byron finally managed to grab the blade, but not before receiving a nasty slash on his forearm.

Seeing what she had done, a semblance of reality had flitted across Lina's gentle features. She grabbed what few belongings she had at Byron's Vancouver apartment and stormed out. He never forgot her last words before slamming the door: "You're here but you're not here. You're not emotionally present."

He glanced down at the six-inch scar on his right forearm and sighed. Afterward, he had quit his job as a hospital porter, packed up his things and moved to PEI to begin anew. In reality, he was getting bored with his party animal friends anyway. And his relationships had always ended in disaster.

There were a few others, but those were the memorable ones. And he didn't want to think of the other ones right now anyway. He was slowly becoming depressed thinking about the last three.

And he had vowed to himself that with Akila things would be different. So they had become an item, bought a small house and had two incomes that supported them nicely. They were DINKS—double income, no kids.

The first year was bliss. But the tiger was having difficulty changing his stripes. He had thrown himself into a writing career, finally pursuing his passion and bringing his stories to fruition. Not only was he getting his work published. It was selling and he had a modest following. *But is that everything?*

The closest thing to what Byron would later describe as an epiphany suddenly popped into his head.

*Without love, I have nothing at all.*

*Fucking moron.* He powered down the computer, stood and rubbed his fingers over a dull pain in his forehead. He absently glanced at the calendar: Thursday, August 23$^{rd}$.

An alarm sounded from the far reaches of his memory. Two years to the day that Akila's parents had been murdered. He hadn't said a single word about it to her. And he knew damn well she became depressed on that day. *Insensitive bastard.*

"The least I could have done was plan something special. But, no what do I go and do? Tell her I have some creative inspiration that I would really like to get documented. You stupid fuck. And Susanne's going through hell, and the body of your best friend was just stolen, while you're sitting at your fucking keyboard trying to be creative? Get a life."

The angry soliloquy echoed eerily through the empty old house as Byron ran into the living room and picked up the phone. He dialed Akila and listened to it ring four times before going to voice mail. He hung up without leaving a message and tried again. "Come on ... come on Akila," he said, listening to the rings. It went to voice mail again and he left a message: "Hi, honey, it's me. Listen, I'm sorry for being an insensitive bastard lately. Call me. I'd like to take you to dinner tonight."

He shuffled around the house nervously for a few minutes before deciding to drive over to Susanne's house. Perhaps they were having a heart-to-heart and didn't hear the phone.

A few minutes later, he pulled in front of Susanne's house, noticing immediately that her SUV was not there.

And neither was Akila's Audi.

He screeched to a stop and ran up the concrete walkway. He rang the bell repeatedly as he peered in the window. No one came. The house looked empty.

He raced around into the backyard, reached the garage and peered in a lone wood-framed window. No vehicle inside.

Terrifying thoughts raced through his mind. *Susanne wanted to resurrect Elias. Elias's body was stolen from the funeral home. Eleanor had a knife. She wanted to kill me. What about Susanne and Akila? Has Eleanor got them? What about Elias?*

*If he's been resurrected, will he have the same violent tendencies as Eleanor? He'll try and kill Susanne. And Akila.*

Breathing in short gasps, he ran around to the front street, planning to do a full-scale search.

As he raced to his car, a black Crown Vic rolled down the street and stopped in front of Susanne's house. Bryon ran curbside as the tinted window rolled down. The unshaven and unhappy face of Detective Clay Redmond regarded him. "Looking for somebody?"

"Yeah ... Akila and Susanne."

"Susanne is missing. So is Riley. When was the last time you talked to Akila?"

"A ... a few hours ago. She told me she was coming here."

"Susanne went missing last night. Did you call Akila?"

Byron nodded. "She doesn't answer. It's not like her."

The detective hesitated. His vacation plans would have to be put on hold. *Shit. First Eleanor appears, then Riley goes missing, then Elias goes missing—or appears—then Susanne goes missing. What the hell is going on? Now Akila. Fuck.*

"Get in."

"What?"

"You want to find her don't you?"

"Of course." The pain in his head intensified, slowly spreading its punishing tendrils.

"Well get the fuck in the car."

Byron climbed in the front seat next to Redmond and closed the door.

"Tell me where you think Akila might be. We'll do a search."

# Chapter Seventeen

"They'll do a search. You can't get away with this," Akila said as Riley's fishing vessel chugged along a few hours later in calm, still waters. Wearing a spaghetti-strap white blouse, hunter-green shorts and leather sandals, she twisted her legs, trying to free herself from the ties that constrained her. It was no use. The plastic zip-ties only cinched tighter, pinching skin. She was curled on deck in a fetal position eyeing her captors nervously.

"It'll be much too late by the time they do a search," Eleanor said, while Elias navigated the vessel closer to Gordon's Island. "We'll be done by then. Mission accomplished."

"You'll never get away with this."

"Quiet now ... little Twinkie. Your time to speak will come." Eleanor's eyes were far away.

Akila shifted around so her head faced the control room. She saw the back of Elias's head steering toward the tiny islands. "Elias ... Elias, help me. You don't want to do ..."

Eleanor stuffed a stinky sock in Akila's mouth and taped it securely with duct tape. "Keep your mouth shut, buttercup. There are other boats around."

A few fishing vessels passed and the respective crews exchanged waves in the crimson light of dusk. Elias glanced back for a second and returned his attention to steering.

Akila started to hyperventilate. She focused all her energy and took deep breaths, remembering a metaphor her grief counselor had taught her after the tragic death of her parents. *You are floating high in the sky, on a bright sunny day, looking down contentedly on an infinite vista of mountains, lakes and lush green forests. You see a clump of puffy white clouds and float lazily on top of one. You become one with the cloud, comfortable, calm, serene, floating over a world that you have dominion over. You are the master of your soul, the deity of your destiny. You control your feelings. You are the cloud. Become the cloud—puffy, white, omniscient and ... calm ... calm. Think of a plan to escape.*

A hard kick in the ribs jarred her out of the meditative trance. "Wake up, creampuff. We're here."

Eleanor and Elias carried her onto the beach and dumped her onto the sand. She rolled, landed on her back and took stock of the situation. *What the hell are they going to do to me?*

The sun, now cresting over the forest canopy, glowed bright orange as it slowly disappeared. It was getting dark.

Riley, a blank zombie-like stare in his eyes, approached from the forest. Three sets of faraway eyes studied her slender frame writhing in the sand. The waves gently lapped ashore.

She stared at the eyes, glowing yellowish-red. "What do you want with me? Let me go. I won't tell anybody."

Slowly the images above her transformed into ... what, pirates? Draped in black capes, the signature pirate hats, black swashbuckling boots, they studied Akila. A misty, swirling haze slowly descended from the sky and morphed into Captain Samuel Longhorn.

His subordinates stiffened to attention at the ceremonious arrival of their leader.

He knelt down in front of Akila, ripped the duct tape from her mouth and extracted the stinky sock. She coughed and took a few deep breaths.

"I'm glad you could come, my little princess."

She tried to wriggle away. "What do you want with me?"

But for his yellowish-red eyes, Longhorn glowed black, a silver translucent mist surrounding his body. His eyes darted to the sky, rolled around and returned to the sand. "Guess there's no harm in telling her?" He turned to the others.

They nodded in unison.

"You see, we made a deal with the devil hundreds of years ago. Our ship full of booty was sinking. We didn't want to lose the booty so we made the deal. Satan would protect the loot if we agreed to stay with the ship." He waved a hand out to sea at the fiery image of the phantom ship.

"We sold our souls to the devil. Now we want them back. So, he says bring me thirty more, and once they're dead, you will be resurrected in their bodies, to walk the Earth eternally, immortalized. A soul for a soul, an eye for an eye, a pound of flesh for a pound of flesh."

Akila blinked in terrified confusion. Was she really seeing this, really hearing this? But the dark figures silhouetted against the coming moonlight, the fiery mass far out at sea and the wicked angular face of Captain Samuel Longhorn staring down at her provided enough assurance. This was no nightmare. No, this was actually happening. And unless she thought quickly, she would be very dead very soon. And be resurrected as what ... an eighteenth-century pirate, for fuck sakes?

"So ... you decided instead of just waiting for people to die, you'd go ahead and kill them?"

"The process of waiting for the right ones was becoming painfully slow. We've been floating at sea in that ship for too long. We've run out of patience. Besides, killing has always been a pastime of ours. We're good at it."

"Once you've got your thirty, then what?"

"The phantom ship disappears forever and we walk the Earth." Pointing to the other three pirates, "We walk the Earth at times in our own bodies and ... when the need arises, we transform into the bodies of those who were ... resurrected."

"You'll never get away with this."

"Oh, but we have. We are. I'm afraid you do not understand the true power of the devil, my dear. But you will."

"So, you're going to kill me?"

"You'll have a new life ... a life of immortality."

"It won't be me."

"At times it will."

Akila gritted her teeth and narrowed her eyes at the man in charge. *Stall, stall ... so you can make a plan.* "Byron and Redmond will come for me. You'll never get away with this."

Longhorn eyed her as if she was a misbehaving child. "Don't worry about them coming to rescue you. We've already thought of that. And we have plans to contain them. But enough idle banter. We have a little ceremony planned, my dear. And for that we need a few more invited guests. It's the devil's orders." He waved a hand. "Take her away."

Two of the blackly robed men carried Akila down a small path in the forest, finally stopping at the entrance to a dark cave. She struggled futilely to escape the powerful captors. The ties cinched tighter, pinching skin painfully. They grunted, set her down for a minute, opened a steel door and then picked her up and carried her down a dark tunnel for about twenty feet. It opened to a larger, dimly lit open cave perhaps fifty feet round with a ceiling that disappeared into the darkness. It was impossible to see how high the ceiling was.

They placed her in the middle of a candlelit pentagram, tossed an old musty blanket on top of her and left, but not before sealing shut the rusted metal door.

The candlelit room slowly grew quiet as the retreating footsteps faded. Akila sat up and gazed around the room, at each flickering candle marking the points of the pentagram. She shuddered, but not from the cold.

What kind of a demonic nightmare had she found herself in? *And how the hell am I going to get out of here?*

# Chapter Eighteen

"We can't go in here."

"Sure we can. It's dark, and there's no one around."

"I know but I'm scared."

"Don't be," twenty-three-year old Jimmy Styles encouraged his girlfriend, Debbie Seagram.

He had just pulled into the parking lot of East Point Lighthouse. They had been dating four months to the day, and Jimmy wanted to get laid. Sure, he had done some heavy petting with Debbie before—she had even given him a nice hand job once—but they had never gone all the way. And, his friends, who knew he was a virgin, were starting to tease him about it.

"Jimmy can't close the deal ... Jimmy can't get off first base ... Jimmy will have a lifelong and intimate relationship with the palm sisters ... maybe Jimmy's actually queer and doesn't like girls at all."

It was starting to bother him. Sure, he could just lie, tell them he fucked her. But it wasn't that easy and he knew it. They shared many of the same friends, hung around in the same circles. It would come full circle. They would find out. Then in addition to teasing him about not getting laid, he would also get teased and ridiculed for being a bullshitter. And Jimmy might be a lot of things, but a bullshitter he was not.

He pointed the vehicle toward the lighthouse, parked and shut off the ignition. A small flame flickering out at sea went unnoticed by the lovebirds.

He stared into Debbie's eyes for a moment before brushing a lock of her wavy brown hair away from her face. He slowly traced his finger down her soft cheek, across her dainty nose and along her full lips. Then he pressed his lips to hers and kissed her while the other hand started undoing the buttons of her white blouse.

He felt a tingle. He was getting aroused. Tonight's the night.

Debbie resisted at first but as his other hand slowly wandered down to the mound between her legs, rubbing the tight, indented V in her blue jeans in a slow and steady motion, a soft moan escaped her lips.

"Don't, Jimmy. Not here."

But her actions said something else. Knowing how clumsy he was at undoing her bra, she moved her hands around and unclasped it. She let the white lace bra drop to her legs. Large, full breasts stared him in the face, protruding nipples jutting out like tiny spears.

His mouth moved quickly to the breasts, sucking, kissing and licking the nipples, gently massaging, kneading the firmness in his hand. Definitely more than a mouthful and definitely more than a handful. It took two of his rather large hands to properly support one of her delicious melons.

She let out a soft moan, absently opening her eyes at the flickering lighthouse lantern. Then she saw it. A grinning, flaming face with red eyes appeared in the lantern room, watching her, smiling wickedly, seemingly enjoying the show.

"Wait."

Jimmy removed his mouth from the midnight snack with a slurping sound. Spittle dribbled down his chin. He wiped it away. "What?"

Debbie's eyes were wide. She pointed to the lighthouse. "Look."

He followed her arm. "I don't see any ..."

But then he could make it out—the wickedly grinning face, large horns protruding out at odd angles like the antlers of a deer.

She started buttoning her blouse. "You see it?"

"Yeah."

"Let's get out of here."

"I want to go check it out." Jimmy was fascinated with the paranormal.

"What?"

"Let's go check it out."

Debbie raised an eyebrow, the color draining from her face. "I'm not going in there. You must be crazy. It's locked anyway."

"Why don't I just go take a look? I'll be right back."

Before she could say anything, he was out of the car. He popped open the trunk, and stood at the driver side with a crowbar.

"What are you doing with that?"

"It's just for protection. Lock the doors, roll up the windows. Give me five minutes, okay?"

Debbie slowly nodded. She shivered and rubbed her arms, trying to wipe away the crop of goose bumps that had quickly sprouted. "Don't be long."

"I'm just going to check it out. I won't be long." With a wink and a wry grin, "When I get back we'll go somewhere more comfortable, okay? I have the perfect spot. It's a house with no one around."

With gritted teeth, she nodded. She wasn't sure she wanted to go all the way with Jimmy tonight, but the pleasurable sensation emanating from the wet spot on her crotch was maintaining a position much different from that of her mind. *Maybe tonight's the night.*

He turned and walked toward the lighthouse. She watched his muscular six-foot-four frame become smaller.

Jimmy's interest in the paranormal had gotten the better of him. Maybe, a belief in ghosts gave him hope that indeed we do go somewhere after we die. He didn't buy the religious beliefs his parents had rammed down his throat from a young age, so this was something that would go a long way to giving him a sense that there was life after death. Ghosts. Cool. He had never seen a ghost, but knew the island was rich in ghost stories, folklore and legend. Hell, there were dozens of reportedly haunted houses on the island, even some business establishments. Wouldn't his doubting Thomas friends think he were really cool if he could tell them he saw a ghost? They'd have to believe him. Debbie could back it up. She saw it too.

He reached the door in the moonlit darkness and grabbed the handle. It creaked open. It wasn't even locked.

He took a few deep breaths, glanced back at the car. Satisfied that Debbie was safe, he entered.

He raised the crowbar. "Anyone here?" He listened. The gentle lapping of waves. A crow screeched, soaring overhead in the midnight sky. And then, silence.

"Anyone here?"

Nothing.

He ascended the circular stairs, slowly feeling his way in the dark. Beams of moonlight seeping through the windows suffused the lighthouse with a dim light that, by the time he reached the lantern room, his eyes had adjusted to.

He stood in the lantern room watching the steady and rhythmic light from the beacon that helped navigate seafaring vessels. There was no movement, no sounds, no apparitions of any kind. He was almost disappointed.

He peered out the window at his yellow four-door sedan, could barely make out the attractive face of Debbie. She had turned the interior light on and he thought she was smiling.

He waved. "Hi baby."

He looked out at the dark sea, scanning the ocean waters glowing silvery in the moonlight. He was about to descend the stairs when he stopped. Something caught his eye. He spun around, peered out the window to sea.

The ghost ship lolled gently in the waters, not a hundred yards away, glowing eerie orange as a massive fire engulfed it, the flames dancing and licking at the sky.

"Wow, that's fucking co ..."

*Swoosh.*

He reflexively brought hand to chest. A fountain of warm blood squirted out as his hands clasped the cold steel of a sword that had penetrated his heart. He gasped for breath but all that escaped was a slow gurgling sound as his lungs filled with blood.

His eyes went wide and lifeless. "Whaaaaaaaaaaa ..."

Jimmy Styles dropped to the ground with a loud smacking sound, breathed a breath that sounded something like the sound of gargling with Scope mouthwash and twitched.

Samuel Longhorn extracted the sword, wiped the blade on Jimmy's jeans and sheathed it. He smiled as Jimmy's body twitched spasmodically for a second or two before there was nothing, No more breath. No more movement. No more life.

*Another conquest. I don't need followers to kill for me. I can do it myself. I didn't know Satan had given me that power. This feels good.*

In the car, Debbie saw the dark silhouette of Jimmy for a moment and then his head disappeared, followed by a distant thud. *Or was that a thud? Is my mind playing tricks on me? He'll be back. For sure.*

Hands clasped together tightly, she waited for what seemed eons. But, according to the digital dashboard clock, it had been exactly three minutes and thirty-seven seconds. But, wait. He had been gone longer than ten minutes in total. *He said five minutes. Jimmy's always been punctual. What should I do?*

She agonized over it another minute and then decided. She would drive up to the door of the lighthouse, roll the window down and call him. If he didn't come, well, she would cross that bridge once she arrived. Truth be told, she was scared shitless.

She could sense some dark cloud enveloping the tiny cape on which the lighthouse stood. As if to reinforce the creepy sensation, a misty gray blanket of clouds slowly drifted shoreward. She couldn't describe the sensation if she wanted to, other than to call it pure and unadulterated evil, a force so powerful she felt the very real and physical pain of depression—the tip of a malignant sword scratching at her mind.

*Just start the car, get the fuck out of here. Fuck plan A. Fuck plan B. Proceed directly to plan C. Do not pass go, do not collect two hundred dollars.*

But Debbie ignored the voice of reason, started the car, drove over and stopped abruptly at the front door. She rolled down the window with a trembling hand. "JJJJJJJJ ... Jimmy. Let's get out of here. Jimmy, let's get out of here. JIMMY, LET'S GET THE FUCK OUT OF HERE ... NO ..."

The glinting metal blade glided smoothly through the open window, sliced through jugular vein and severed Debbie's head clean off—decapitated.

It flew onto the back seat, bounced twice and rolled into a passenger door while her body twitched and blood squirted from her neck like a garden sprinkler.

The acrid copper smell of fresh blood—and plenty of it—permeated the air and invaded Samuel's expectant nostrils. Watching the spectacle of death, he inhaled deeply and smiled. "I love the smell of blood in the evening. Next."

# Chapter Nineteen

"What next? What the fuck do I do next?" Byron paced the floor of his house the next afternoon out of his mind with worry and stress. He hadn't slept a wink last night. He and Redmond had combed the area, driven around the countryside, visiting a few local beaches, even returning to East Point Lighthouse.

But nothing.

Not a trace of Akila. They had no clue where she might be. And equally disturbing, Riley and Susanne had vanished mysteriously without a trace. Not to mention the missing corpse of Elias. Something had to be done. It was his fault. All his fault. Overcome with the need, the desire, the all-consuming passion to create. Was it an addiction like the newly coined Facebook Addiction Disorder? They had specialized psychologists for that. Were there specialists for writing addiction?

He didn't know. But he knew it had so far cost him the woman he wanted to spend the rest of his life with. And that sucked. Big time.

Balling his fists, he stopped pacing, stared at the kitchen tabletop—as if the answer to all his problems were contained somewhere within the woodgrain pattern—and hammered his fist down hard. The table shook and a glass of water tipped over, rolled off the table, exploding as it hit the floor, a sinister symbol of how quickly his world was shattering into smithereens.

He studied the glittering glass fragments, the water dripping onto the terracotta tile floor. Redmond said he would call this morning. It was already one-thirty in the afternoon and he hadn't heard from the seasoned and cynical detective. What happened to him?

He went into the living room, slumped into the leather couch and picked up his cell phone. First he tried Akila's number. Four rings and then voice mail. How many messages had he left? Ten maybe? Ten at least. Probably more like fifteen. He found the detective's cell number in his contact list and dialed.

On three rings, Redmond picked up. "Yeah?"

"Detective Redmond ..."

"Clay, for fuck sakes. My subordinates have to call me Detective Redmond ... and even they don't do that. You're a fucking civilian."

Something had pissed off *Clay* today.

"Sorry, Clay. Do you have any news on Akila?"

"No, I don't. Have you been watching the news?"

"No."

"Well, I've got two more missing persons on my radar today. I'm not a fucking happy camper."

"Two more?"

"Yeah ... couple kids disappeared at East Point Lighthouse last night. A lot of blood but no bodies."

"You there now?"

"Yeah ... listen, Byron, I'll be honest with you. I've got a shitload of detective work to do today and I was supposed to be leaving on a plane for vacation. Do you know how long it's been since I've had a holiday?"

Byron knew the man casually. He had had coffee with him on four separate occasions at the local Tim Hortons. While they were on friendly terms, the relationship could hardly be called a friendship. He didn't want to push the detective's buttons, ruin his chances of spending another day with him, searching for Akila.

"No, but I imagine it's been a long time."

"Three fucking years is a very long time, my friend."

Maybe he was wrong about the friendship part. "Listen, I'm sorry to bother you, det ... ah Clay, but I feel completely useless, worried sick about Akila. Would you mind if I tagged along with you for a while, maybe exchange theories about all this weird shit?"

Redmond was about to blast him, but precipitously had a change of heart. A flashback seared through his mind, the day two years ago when his wife had died. He had taken his eyes off her for two seconds, and she had been riddled with machine gun fire by a murderer posing as a Canadian combat soldier. Of course, he had taken the law into his own hands and deposited a bullet through the head of the murderer. But that didn't change the fact he still had a soft spot for someone who was sick with worry and grief about a missing girlfriend. Especially since that someone felt responsible. He was all too familiar with that gnawing feeling of emptiness and guilt.

And, hell, he often bent the rules anyway. It had become his new modus operandi. "I'll pick you up in an hour."

Byron changed into hiking boots, jeans, navy blue kangaroo jacket and a black baseball cap. He had no idea where the search would take them. But he wanted to be prepared for anything. He contemplated bringing his Glock but at the last minute changed his mind. The handgun had been acquired illegally for protection. He knew it was insane, but one of his horror novels had left him with such a ruinous feeling after completing the book that he had purchased the handgun through a friend of a friend who had a connection with a seedy gang-banger. After writing the novel about the demented serial killer stalking and murdering men and women, Byron had become unnecessarily convinced he was next on the psycho's list—even though the character was a figment of his imagination.

*No, better leave the piece here.*

Redmond might not take too kindly to seeing an illegal firearm in spite of his reputation for lawlessness.

And, he didn't know him well enough to risk it. He returned the handgun to its safe spot underneath the mattress and waited downstairs in the living room, still pacing and occasionally pulling the sheer window coverings back and peering out the bay window.

As soon as he saw the Crown Vic turn down the quiet side street, he was out the door and standing curbside. Redmond screeched to a stop and Byron got in.

Redmond regarded him with narrow eyes. "Do you know how to use a handgun?"

"Yeah."

He handed him a Glock nine millimeter. "Here. You might need it. This stays between you and me."

Byron stuffed it in the crotch of his jeans without asking questions. He had other things on his mind. "Where are we off to?"

"Montague. Report of a domestic disturbance."

"We're not looking for Akila?"

The detective bristled. "Listen, you signed up for this. I have to take care of something first."

Byron only nodded as Redmond weaved his way through traffic.

As they reached Highway 1 eastbound, Byron told Redmond his theory. He explained his nightmares of shooting people and how immediately afterward they sprang back to life. He told him about the lighthouse, how he felt it was in some way connected to the resurrections, missing people and corpse theft. He finished by saying his nightmares had foretold the events. He often had dreams that came true.

"Premonition dreams I've heard it called," Byron said.

Redmond scratched his stubble, ran a hand through his thick red hair. He extracted a tiny cigar and popped it in his mouth. "Do you mind?"

Byron shook his head.

Redmond lit up and continued. "So you think all this stuff was foretold in your dreams?"

Byron nodded.

"That's some fucked up dreams you've been having."

"I've got a fucked up psyche. I'm a writer."

Redmond stared at Byron curiously, rolled down his window and blew a cloud of smoke into the wind. "I guess artists are usually bent in one way, shape or form."

"A lot of times we just process information differently."

"Yeah, in your conscious and your sub-conscious."

Byron wanted to steer the conversation away from writing. Lately, thinking about it just brought him grief. It was that preoccupation that had created the situation with Akila—a missing persons file.

"Do you have any theories on what's going on here?"

The detective took a long drag, blew out another cloud of smoke and looked at Byron. "It's clear the lighthouse is in some way connected. So are Riley and Susanne. I think they broke into the funeral home and stole Elias's body. I don't know what you guys saw with Eleanor. I visited the gravesite yesterday and it's hard to say if it's been disturbed. Everything looked to be as it should be. But, the recent rains washed away some of the topsoil so really it was inconclusive."

"We saw her in the flesh. Riley must've dug up her body."

"Well, it's not that easy for me to dig up that grave site. Lots of bureaucratic red tape. And we don't have time for that right now. Can you tell me anything you might have missed?"

Byron scratched a two-day growth, adjusted the baseball cap and thought about it. After a minute, he said, "I noticed that when we went to the lighthouse the mannequin had been disturbed."

"Disturbed?"

"Yeah. At first it was staring at the wall. I looked at it a little later and the head was staring straight up at the ceiling. No one had been in the room."

Redmond knew instinctively there was more. He didn't say anything.

"Have you heard the story about the phantom ship?"

Redmond nodded. "Almost everyone has."

"I think it's somehow connected."

"That's fucking folklore." As the words left Redmond's lips his contemplative expression gave away a different viewpoint. His words lacked conviction.

"Call it what you want, I think it's tied into this."

"Well, all I know is if I don't come up with some answers, and soon, my captain is going to put my nuts in a blender. He says if I don't have some solid leads by the end of today, he's calling in reinforcements from other jurisdictions. He thinks this is way beyond the scope of our little police force."

"What do you think?"

"I think he's full of shit. And I intend to prove it. Hang on ..."

Redmond's cell phone rang and he answered. After a short conversation, he hung up and turned toward Byron, pulling onto Main Street, Montague. "Things have gotten a little out of hand here."

"How so?"

"There a woman, Mila Slovanovich, says her husband is behaving strangely. Trying to take her on a boat trip somewhere. He hates boats, hates the water."

"What's he doing living on an island then?"

"Never mind. Anyway, she refused the boat trip and he wacked her over the head with a beer bottle. Apparently she's holed up in her bathroom petrified."

"What do you want me to do?"

"Stay in the car."

They pulled down Ricky Street, parked in front of a pink wood frame two-story home. Redmond exited and scratched his head. He knew it was crazy, but he said it anyway. "On second thought, wait across the street, behind that van over there. Keep your eyes open."

Byron got out. "Where's all the other cops?"

"Looking for three missing persons and at least three missing dead bodies." He turned and marched down the path to the front door.

Redmond knocked on the door a few times and waited. Nothing. He rang the doorbell three times and still heard nothing. On an impulse, he went into the back yard and approached from the rear. He walked up the wooden stairs onto the small porch and peered in the window of the rear screen door. He saw a rotund man with a bald head standing outside a bathroom door, a claw hammer concealed in a hand behind his back, the other hand knocked softly on the door. He pleaded for his wife to come out.

Redmond had been briefed. Rennie and Mila Slovanovich were the owners of the home. Apparently Rennie hadn't been behaving normally today. Of all days, Redmond sighed. He slowly opened the back door. Fuck police protocol. He had never let it get in the way before. Well, maybe there was a time when protocol would have come first. But, now that his wife Shawna was dead, protocol could go straight to hell for all he cared.

Rennie stared vacantly at Redmond. He raised the hammer.

"Whooah there, cowboy. I wouldn't do that if I were you."

Rennie stepped forward, arcing the hammer high in the air. His eyes were maniacal.

Redmond drew his gun, leveling it at the man. "Drop the hammer and put your hands in the air."

A muffled scream echoed from behind the bathroom door. "Take him away from here. He's gone crazy."

Rennie's gaze diverted from Redmond and glanced for a split second at the bathroom door. It was all the time Redmond needed. He slid the Glock into its holster and charged forward, tackling Rennie to the floor and wrestling for control of the hammer.

Rennie outweighed Redmond's frame by about a hundred pounds. And Redmond was out of shape, the result of a one-year alcoholic binge that in his mind helped him cope with Shawna's murder. He carried about twenty pounds of beer belly. The cancer sticks only exacerbated matters.

They hit the wooden floor hard, Redmond landing on top of Rennie. From the bottom, Rennie raised the hammer and Redmond grabbed his meat hook in both hands. He was no match for Rennie's strength. The hammer inched slowly toward his head. Rennie jerked suddenly and bounced Redmond off.

Rennie rolled over, pulled the hammer free, and sat his heavy bulk on Redmond's chest.

In the bathroom, Mila screamed and pounded on the door.

Rennie swung the hammer down hard and Redmond instinctively slid his head to the side. It slammed into the wooden floor with a hollow echo, narrowly avoiding staining the refinished hardwoods with blood and brain matter.

*Fuck. This guy's bat shit crazy.*

Rennie raised the hammer again, eyes glazed over—lifeless and unfocused. He could have been watching a soap opera.

Redmond heard the door creak, saw a man sprinting down the hallway. Rennie glanced behind and Byron tackled him, knocking him off Redmond and sending the hammer flying through the air. It hit the drywall with a loud thud and clattered along the floor.

Byron grasped Rennie from behind with both hands. Rennie grunted and stood up, Byron riding piggy-back. Redmond grabbed his gun, took two quick steps and cracked the ape hard over the head with the butt end. He dropped like a lead balloon with a face-plant onto the hardwood, Byron still clinging to his back.

Redmond holstered the weapon, ignoring the blood dripping from its grip. "Thanks for that."

Panting for breath, Byron unhooked himself from the ape, stood up and nodded his head.

Rennie was out cold.

Redmond cuffed him, waved Byron outside and approached the screaming bathroom door. After some coaxing, Mila opened the door and entered the hallway, staring at her unconscious husband. She was a waif of a woman, dressed in a one-piece mid-length black cotton dress that stopped just short of her bony kneecaps.

Crack cocaine was the first thought that entered Redmond's mind, but he ignored it. "We're putting him in lock-up for the night."

She brushed away a few tears and nodded. "He's crazy. I don't know what got into him. He went for a walk earlier today, returned and tried to talk me into going on a boat trip."

"Did he say where?"

She brushed a few strands of thin hair away from her gaunt face. "Murray Islands."

"What's out there?"

"He didn't say."

At that point two uniformed police officers entered. Local Montague cops. They didn't look too impressed. He had unceremoniously stepped into their turf without so much as a courtesy call. Another breach of protocol. Redmond had a tense conversation with them and left.

He had better things to do than sort out the details of a domestic disturbance, or attempted murder for that matter. He knew it was in some way connected to the disappearance of Riley, Akila and Susanne. Real people in real danger were far more pressing right now. He would follow it up later.

"Where are we going now?" Byron asked as they drove away.

"Girl Guide Road."

"What's there?"

"I'm going to see a man about a boat. Then, we're taking a cruise to Murray Islands. I have a gut instinct on this one."

"What about police backup?"

"Fuck backup. Half the force thinks I'm crazy anyway."

# Chapter Twenty

*I'm going crazy. This shit isn't happening.* Akila writhed around on the rocky floor of the dark cave, but it was no use. She could barely move. She was curled up, hands securely tied behind her back with plastic zip-ties, her ankles bound together with the same restraints. A chunk of cotton had been placed in her mouth, along with a fresh piece of duct tape to secure it in place. She had spent the night tossing and turning, trying to formulate an escape plan, and worrying about how much longer she had to live. She had barely slept, and when she did manage to drift off she had abruptly awakened by agonizing screams. It was impossible to tell if the screams were coming from inside her head or someone was being tortured.

Riley, delivering helpless victim after helpless victim into the cave, had also disrupted shut-eye attempt.

On one such unwelcome visit, he dragged a bound and gagged victim, strategically placed the young woman clad only in pink panties and a white lace bra at the tip of one of the five points of the pentagram, which had been roughly inscribed into the surface with some black chalky substance.

While leaving the terrified female victim, he had stopped suddenly, and with beady eyes glowing yellow-orange in the dimly lit chamber, regarded Akila with a twisted, perverted stare. "You're attractive," he had said. "But you'd be much more so without your clothes." He produced a knife, approached, slashed her clothes to shreds and stood gawking at her semi-nude body, a tent growing in the crotch of his coveralls, before spinning around and leaving.

Now, she wore only a pair of white lace panties and her shivering body crawled with goose bumps, erect nipples on large breasts contradicting the reality that she was as far from sexually aroused as she had ever been in her life.

Realizing her eyes were squeezed shut—in a state of denial—she slowly opened them and, for the umpteenth time, took stock of her surroundings. About a dozen candles lit the extremities of the cave, placed in rock outcrops. Individual candles also marked the five points of the pentagram and a metal urn of sorts stood in the middle with a wooden-handled torch pointing up, flickering and faintly illuminating the other victims, one at each of the points. She stared at the small yellow flame dancing in the candle a few feet away from her head for a moment before sweeping her gaze around the pentagram at the other bound and gagged victims.

She registered their wide eyes, glowing yellow from the flame's reflection and knew. They were terrified. A bra-and-panty clad female victim beside her grunted. She turned her head. Tears streamed down the young woman's petrified face. The woman twisted in the dirt, reaching a position where her feet pointed at a candle a few feet away.

What was she doing? Akila grunted back. She didn't know what else to do. Then she realized, the woman, pointing her toes at the candle, intended to use its flame to burn the plastic zip-ties binding her ankles.

Maybe it was a good idea? Akila stared at the small candle beside her and considered following suit. Did she have any better ideas? No.

The woman wriggled her body close to the flame near the pentagram point. She kicked her bound ankles up and, sliding closer, slowly lowered them to within an inch or so from the candle.

A muffled scream escaped from her gag as the flames began melting plastic and burning skin, a line of black smoke twirling up. She jerked away from the flame, gasping as fresh tears streamed down her face, and repositioned ankles on flames.

Four pairs of glowing eyes watched.

She winced as the flames burned a second time. There was a snapping sound as the plastic melted and her ankles burst into flames. She frantically twisted her legs and smothered the flame. Ignoring the burns, she stood up for a moment. She swept her gaze around the cave to the grunts and groans of the other victims. She finally stared at the torch burning in the center, approached and extended bound wrists into the flame. She grimaced, but with resolve borne of the need to survive, kept them there until the flaming plastic melted.

She jumped back. Burning rivulets of fire snaked down her arms. She dove to the ground, rolling, wiping her arms along the gravelly floor and smothering the flames. She stood up, ripped the duct tape away from her mouth and gritted her teeth to prevent a scream. Covered in dust and first-degree burns, her sweeping gaze regarded the other prisoners.

They squirmed, grunted and groaned.

She advanced toward Akila and stopped abruptly at the sound of a creaking iron door opening.

"Mmmmmmmmff, mmmmmmmmfff," Akila grunted, rolling her eyeballs to the spot beside the one empty pentagram point. Akila wanted her to curl up and feign captivity.

But it was too late. Riley had spotted her.

He dropped a bound male victim, another sacrificial lamb in the macabre demonic ritual, and quickly advanced into the cave. He extracted a large knife and attacked.

In her panic the woman, her long black hair flowing behind an athletic body, tripped over one of the bound victims and fell to the ground.

With one hand, Riley jerked her up violently by the hair and plunged the knife deep in her throat. She gurgled and spewed a fountain of blood as he quickly extracted it, sliced her throat for good measure, dragged her to the center of the pentagram and tossed her dead body beside the flaming torch.

"Let that be a lesson to any of you who tries to escape," he said, wiping the blade on his coveralls and tucking the knife back into a side pocket.

The victims groaned. Terrified muffled screams echoed inside hell on Earth.

# Chapter Twenty-One

*Earth to Susanne. Earth to Susanne. Come in Susanne. Come back to reality, girl.*

She couldn't muster the courage to leave the small cave for two, three days now. She didn't know how long, she had completely lost track of time, the darkness obscuring the ticking seconds, minutes, hours, days and years by which we define, compartmentalize and order our lives.

She had heard footsteps, gut-wrenching screams piercing the still night air, and become almost catatonic with fear. She had crawled deep into the cave, curled up and froze; at times drifting into a horror-filled state of semi-sleep, conscious that at any moment she could be rudely awakened and brutally executed to be used as a pawn in an evil plot to resurrect people from the dead.

Her only company, and she was thankful for it, was Robbie the Raccoon. On a few occasions, he had lumbered up to her in the dark, his yellow eyes glowing curiously, nestled comfortably beside her and fallen asleep. She had even started stroking him affectionately a few times. Initially he had resisted, hissed angrily, but after a while the little critter must have realized she meant no harm and acquiesced, allowing Susanne to gently stroke his small furry head and body. On one occasion, he had snuggled so close to her, they were spooning each other for a few hours, before Robbie disappeared into the night to do whatever raccoons do.

Susanne had gotten used to his schedule, his comings and goings. When he turned in for the night, or whenever he slept, she didn't know if it was night or day, she would try and do the same. The only difference was Robbie was actually sleeping while Susanne remained in some dreadful halfway point between conscious and the unconscious; a twisted, surreal and terrifyingly hallucinogenic reality.

But she had grown tired, weary, thirsty and hungry. And, after much soul-searching, she decided she would rather die in a fight for her life than curled up like some coward in a fetal position in Robbie's humble abode.

She knew, like dead fish, house guests start to stink after three days. Robbie had been hospitable, falling just short of rolling out the red carpet treatment. Maybe in his mind it was the red carpet treatment?

There was no point in overstaying her welcome.

She giggled at the thought. "Robbie, are you getting tired of me? Are you going to kick me out? Am I starting to stink like a rotting dead fish?"

The words echoed hollowly in the cave until an eerie silence enveloped the small space and Susanne's depleted senses.

*Earth to Susanne. Come in, nutcase.*

She twisted around, her atrophied muscles slowly and painfully obeying brain commands. She crawled up to the entrance, pushing away a few tree branches, an attempt at camouflage, scrambled outside and looked around.

*Thanks for the hospitality, Robbie.*

The sky was an orange haze, the crimson sun only partially visible as it set below a canopy of trees in the distance. It was dusk. She untied her blue sweatshirt wrapped around her waist—a makeshift blanket during the night—and pulled it over a pink t-shirt.

*Water. I need water.*

Taking the path from whence she came, she moved toward the ocean, to the distant sounds of voices growing nearer. After a few minutes, she reached the edge of the forest and peered out at the beach. The winds had begun to increase as a large gray mass of clouds slowly descended on the tiny island. Large waves crashed ashore and a dozen or so boats rocked violently in the water, some tied to a makeshift wooden dock.

A tall dark figure stood around a group of six. Wearing a pirate's hat and waving around a large sword, he barked out orders to his followers. With a pang of emotion, she recognized Elias in the mix.

Two bound and gagged bodies lay on the sand, motionless but for the odd twitch of protestation.

"It's almost time," Captain Samuel Longhorn said, before the wind caught the words and carried them out to sea. "Take them away."

The followers lifted the bodies and the procession moved down the beach toward what appeared to be another trail leading somewhere else.

The only thing on Susanne's mind was escape.

When the procession disappeared out of sight, she rallied what strength remained and darted to the dock. She leaped into a lolling speed boat and jumped into the driver seat.

She scanned the dashboard. "Shit ... where the fuck are the keys?"

She leaped up, quickly scanning the boat's floor. An orange-painted sponge shaped like a boat protruded from a side compartment. She pulled it out. Two keys dangled from a small keychain attached to it. She sat down, inserted the key and turned it. It turned over a few times and sputtered. *Come on you fucking thing. START!*

Thunder rumbled from the heavens. A prickly finger of lightening exploded downward, sizzled and cracked as it struck a nearby boat. Thunder bellowed again and a thick sheet of rain pelted Susanne and the small craft.

She turned the key again. The engine roared to life.

She heard a clunk and spun around. A sharp pain pierced through her skull and warm blood streamed into her eyes. Her vision blurred for a few seconds, grew hazy gray and faded to black. *Thanks for your hospitality, Robbie.*

Riley wiped warm blood from the baseball bat on dirty coveralls, smiled and scratched his cheek.

The plan was taking shape.

# Chapter Twenty-Two

"So is that our plan then?" Byron asked, searching the intent eyes of excommunicated Catholic priest Paul Bishop.

Redmond also searched the man's focused eyes.

They sat around a kitchen table in a modest two-story home about a block from the dock that would take them to Murray Islands. A number of missing person calls and assault reports had delayed their arrival. It was now approaching midnight. The old home heaved and creaked as the fierce storm battered its antiquated frame.

They sat down and the elderly man made a pot of coffee. He had said something about the arrival of the beast with seven heads and ten horns, how they must do everything in their power to stop him and how *he* must play a key role in the destruction of Satan's evil influence.

Redmond had suggested borrowing the old man's converted fishing boat, driving it to the islands, affecting a rescue and somehow a destruction of the evil force that was rocking the tiny island to its very core, threatening to cut an evil swath of carnage through the entire populace.

Violence was exploding everywhere. Police resources were stretched thin.

The old man adjusted horn-rimmed spectacles framing his weathered features and bald head. "And I saw a beast rising up out of the sea, having seven heads and ten horns, and on his horns ten crowns, and on his heads a blasphemous name. From Revelation thirteen, one."

Redmond, although not religious, had consulted the preacher previously on cases involving devil worship. The man's information had proven invaluable. He wasn't about to second-guess him. But, at the same time, he wasn't sure a ninety-two-year-old man should be out in the dangerous storm, let alone he and Byron.

"I don't know, Father. This could be too dangerous for you."

Paul cupped his wrinkled hands on the mug of hot coffee, formed a toothless smile, and took a sip. "The Bible tells us our world will end soon. Now is the time man will choose to worship either God or Satan. The devil is now, recruiting his followers, as foretold in the Bible."

Byron interjected: "But, Father, the seas are rough, this won't be easy."

Through eyes stripped of vitality by the passage of time, Paul's gaze met Byron's eyes. "I am old and if God decides it is my time, then I go to Him willingly in the service of my duty to prevent the spread of evil."

"Are you sure you're up for this?" Redmond asked Byron. "We could wait for the weather to calm."

Paul's eyes had gone far away.

"It might be too late by then," Byron said. He was itching to go—felt that every wasted second could mean the difference between life or death for Akila. Where was Akila? Was she all right?

Paul continued: "If anyone worships the beast and his image and receives his mark on the forehead or on the hand, he, too, will drink of the wine of God's fury, which has been poured full strength into the cup of his wrath. Revelation, 14:9,10."

Byron and Redmond stared at the preacher.

"I will deliver the wrath of God onto all evil," Paul said resolutely. "Let us make haste."

With a swiftness of motion that belied his years, he stood up and strode into a bedroom. He returned a few minutes later dressed in black priest garb, the signature white collar glowing ominously in the diffused light from a few incandescent bulbs.

Byron stared at the priest in disbelief. Paul was dead serious and Byron had taken the preacher to be out of his head.

"Have you seen a ghost? Let's go," Paul said.

Buffeting by strong winds and sheeting rain, they exited the house and Paul led them into an old barn that had been fashioned into a garage. He unlocked a large gun rack, stuffed with an assortment of weapons, AK-47s, handguns, grenades, even a rocket-propelled grenade launcher. He had anticipated this epic war for many years. It had been the reason the church had excommunicated him.

During some sermons, he had encouraged the congregation to "take up arms in a fight against a powerful evil that will soon descend upon you with a violent fury."

Paul peeled the tarp off a speedboat while Redmond instructed Byron on how to fire an AK-47 and use grenades.

Byron listened intently, chilling flashbacks of his nightmares coursing through his adrenaline-infused brain.

Twenty minutes later, they left the small dock at the end of Girl Guide Road.

Paul expertly ploughed the boat through eight-foot swells toward the islands. It rocked violently, frequently twisting off course as the three were battered by rain and intense winds.

The fiery phantom ship was the first thing they saw as the speedboat finally rounded the first island. It glowed brilliantly in the dark sky, defying the rain's effort to douse its fiery brightness. Blood-red eyes danced in the flames, accompanied by mocking shrieks of laughter.

They pulled up to the makeshift dock, tied the boat off and searched the beach, illuminated by the glowing ship.

Byron and Redmond stepped onto the dock.

Byron turned to Paul, who was now standing with arms outstretched in a supplicating gesture to the heavens, uttering an incomprehensible prayer. "Aren't you coming?"

"In time, young son. In time." He resumed the prayer to the rolling of thunder, the crackling and hissing of lightening.

Byron and Redmond stepped onto the sand, watched and listened. But for the drone of Paul's prayer, the cacophony of evil cackles from the phantom ship, the thundering storm, they couldn't see any imminent threat of danger—no enemies.

Then it happened. A guttural growling sound echoed from the tree line. Byron spun around. A two-headed horned beast, fiery red eyes and furry dark head, sprinted toward them, exposing large fangs menacingly as it neared.

Byron didn't waste any time, instantly firing a burst of machine gun fire. The spray penetrated the beast, it grunted and dropped dead.

But more charging—a screaming tide of evil.

Machine gun fire erupted from both weapons, short, clapping bursts that felled the attackers.

Byron, braids of bullets draped over his kangaroo jacket, grenades and handguns strapped to his belt, continued firing.

What?

A downed three-headed monster lifted itself from the sand, the row of bullet holes vanished and it resumed its attack.

*Oh fucking no! My nightmare. My nightmare is coming true.*

Then another one. And another one. And another one.

Soon there were thirty or so beasts charging, large feet slapping in the wet sand, growling ferociously.

"The trees," Redmond said. "Run for cover."

They dashed toward the tree line, howls and growls hot on their heels.

Byron dove behind a small rock outcrop in the trees, trained his weapon and fired. He looked around as approaching beasts grunted, screamed and dropped dead.

Where was Redmond?

"Redmond?"

He continued spraying rounds, watching the enemy drop. Redmond didn't answer and he couldn't see him anywhere. He mowed down a number of beasts and noticed some were slipping into the forest, ducking for cover probably to ambush him later. He heard a staccato burst of machine gun fire behind him and spun around. He could see a yellow flare off in the distance about a hundred yards.

He briefly glanced back at the preacher, who was still standing on the rocking boat, with outstretched hands calling out to the heavens. Predatory beasts surrounded the small boat but, at least for the time being, refused to board it and attack. Paul was being guided by ... God?

The stand-off was silhouetted by the fiery phantom ship. But there was something happening to the flame. It was ... shrinking. Or was it a trick of his rattled mind, an optical illusion borne of adrenaline, nervousness and fear?

Byron didn't know. But he knew he didn't have time for introspection. The dark forest was full of growling predators and the distant bursts of ... surely it was Redmond's machine gun ... echoing in the distance, somewhere near the flaming red flare or torch or whatever the fuck it was.

He spun around, found the small path and hurried along. Let Paul handle the beach invasion. He seemed to be holding off the attackers. None of the beasts dared to climb aboard.

He reached the luminescent flare and realized it was a marker for a cave. A locked metal door blocked the entrance. Redmond was pinned up against a large nearby boulder, blood gushing from a nasty leg wound.

Byron sprayed bullets at two pairs of glowing red eyes in the forest and heard the thud of dead beasts dropping. He knew they wouldn't be dead for long. *Just like my fucking nightmare.*

Redmond bent down with a hand on a ravaged leg. Claws or teeth marks had ripped into it, tearing the fabric of his jeans. A large gash extended from above the knee, down the back of his leg. The fresh wound spurted blood.

The splattered remains of a ... four-headed beast ... lay on the ground beside him, its furry, werewolf-like body bloodied with bullet holes. Byron studied it. Tiny pieces of brain matter crawled along the forest carpet, slowly reassembling on the heads.

The fucking thing was reconstructing itself.

Byron heard a guttural growl. A beast attacked, springing in the air. He riddled it with bullets as it flew. The momentum of its attack sent it tumbling into Byron, knocking him down, landing on top of him. Byron felt warm blood from its chest gush out and drench his body.

He pushed it off, wincing as he noticed one of its claws had imbedded itself in his chest. He plucked a broken claw out and the wound squirted blood.

He returned his attention to Redmond, who was now slumped over, barely conscious from blood loss. So much blood. So much carnage.

He extracted a combat knife, cut a slice of Redmond's jeans and fashioned a tourniquet. As he cinched it tighter, he heard a frantic cry for help.

"Heeeeeeeeeeeeellllllllllllllllllp!"

"Akila?"

He quickly handed Redmond his AK-47 and the detective began firing at attacking monsters.

Byron riddled the iron door with bullets. It creaked open a crack.

Redmond, bracing himself on the rock cave, continued spraying rounds. He waved Byron inside.

Byron pulled the door open and entered. To painful cries of the dead and dying, he extracted a flashlight and slowly moved down the dark tunnel. From behind, he heard the faint, panicked voice of Redmond as the echoing gunfire subsided: "Get off of me, you fucking beast … .aaaaaaaaahhhh."

*Is Redmond dead?* He rounded a bend and heard a voice.

Fiery red eyes stared. "I'm glad you could come. It's not too late."

He recognized the voice of Riley Fitzgerald. But it wasn't really Riley anymore. He was an evil, resurrected servant of Satan.

Riley pulled out a knife and quickly advanced. Byron drew a handgun and shot him twice in the head. He grinned, blood gushing from the double-tap, and dropped dead.

He heard the chants before he saw the light. There was a humming sound echoing from a flame-lit room up ahead. Elias stepped in front of him. "Hi, Byron. Long time, no see."

Byron leveled the machine gun. He uttered a warning even though he knew it was useless. "Step aside or die."

Elias extracted a glittering sword and his features morphed into a fiery horned demon. He opened a mouth exposing large, razor-sharp fangs. "No, you die ..."

Byron plugged his chest with bullets. Elias dropped to the ground with a thud. The sound of bullets ricocheting off cave walls was deafening.

He stepped over the body of his former best friend and into a cavernous hell. Two dark figures sprang out of nowhere, grabbed him by the arms firmly and slammed him into a rock wall. His machine gun dropped and clattered on the ground. He struggled but it was futile. The dark hooded figures—with only glowing red eyes visible—possessed superhuman strength.

He blinked, shuddering as the weight of what was about to unfold enveloped his senses.

In the center of a flaming pentagram, a pile of wood had been gathered. Erected above it was a wooden cross. Akila, completely nude, blood dripping from her extremities, was nailed to the cross. *What? Nailed to a cross?* Alongside the flaming wood pile, sat seven human decapitated heads and ten animal horns, a macabre symbol of the unspeakable evil about to be unleashed.

Samuel Longhorn, glowing blackish-orange, stood beside the cross with a hand-held flaming torch, igniting bits of the kindling. He smiled wickedly.

Five bound and gagged bodies marked the points of the pentagram and darkly hooded servants of Satan surrounded the grisly ritual, chanting an eerie "oooooooooooooooooooooo, aaaaaaaaaaaaaaa" sound.

A demonic choir preparing for a ritual sacrifice to resurrect Satan.

The bodies writhed and moaned but for one. Byron recognized the body of his friend, Susanne. Blood seeped from a head wound and formed a red halo-like puddle around her head. Probably dead.

He grimaced. *Paul was right. Where the fuck is he?*

"No," Byron shouted, struggling with his captors.

"It's a little late for that," Samuel said.

Akila's eyes slowly opened. She stared at Byron, her mouth and eyes wide with terror. "Byron, help me."

He wrestled with his captors and for his trouble received a powerful knee to the nuts. He doubled over and dropped to the ground. He twisted, moaned and writhed in pain.

The chants continued, the flames grew. "God help me," Akila shouted. "God help us all!"

"By the power vested within me, I hereby command you to stop." Father Paul Bishop stood resolutely at the cave entrance with his hands outstretched.

Samuel backed away.

Akila screamed as the flames licked closer to her body.

The chanting stopped. A dark figure approached Paul and he pointed an index finger. A powerful lightning bolt exploded from the finger, struck the attacker, shattering him into a million pieces of ash that floated lazily to the ground.

Byron, still gripping his aching groin, writhing in pain, managed to swing his head around to see the miracle unfold.

Paul approached the center of the pentagram, walked untouched into a swirl of intensifying flames, and freed Akila from what would have been a torturously painful death.

Overcome with pain and fear, she collapsed on the ground outside the flame.

Byron crawled to his machine gun and felt a sharp pain as one of Samuel's minions kicked him hard to the head. His head swam, images blurring.

Samuel moved toward the exit. His fiery eyes had lost their resolve. There was another emotion visible—fear.

"Stop." It was the commanding voice of Father Paul Bishop. He stood atop the fire, backdropped by the flaming cross.

"Do you think you can make a dent in Satan's master plan?" Samuel said. "You're crazy old man. Give it up,"

Paul's clothes caught fire. He pointed an index finger at Samuel. A powerful lightning bolt struck him. He burst into flames and exploded into a million pieces of black ash. A vague silvery image floated up and disappeared.

Paul, now completely engulfed in flames, pointed fingers of fury at the Satan-incarnated followers. One by one, they shrieked, cried, screamed and shattered into dark ash.

The lightning bolts cracked, popped and finally fizzled out. The last thing Byron remembered seeing before passing out was the preacher, strapped to the burning cross—his God-like image a misty white, a barely visible halo floating above his head.

The Father smiled. He had finally found his calling.

An angel in life.

An angel in death.

A savior of mankind—through and through.

# Epilogue

*Through and through,* Byron thought as he watched the fiery sun disappear behind the edge of the water far out at sea. *He was a savior through and through. A good man to the very end—selflessly dedicating his life for the betterment of mankind.*

Akila touched his arm gently. "What are you thinking?"

Byron thought about lying. What was the point? "I was thinking about Paul, about what a great man he was."

Her brilliant green eyes became thoughtful. She touched her dolphin necklace, examining the grinning mammal introspectively for a moment. "Paul saved our lives ... with your help."

Byron studied his own dolphin necklace, looked up and nodded. In swimsuits, they lay together on a large yellow towel three months later on a sandy beach in Punta Cana, Dominican Republic. It had taken some time, but they finally felt healed enough to go on an all-inclusive vacation to the popular tourist destination.

Byron's nightmares had only now started to abate in ferocity and frequency, although he was still haunted by horrific images of shooting Elias. He knew, after three months of psychotherapy, the nightmares would probably never go away. His therapist had told him as much. But, at least he felt better prepared to deal with them. She had armed him with some much-needed coping skills. He felt stronger and more resilient than he had a few months ago.

And while Akila was at her counseling sessions, he had, on the advice of his therapist, resumed writing *Resurrected Souls*.

145

He had finished the first draft. She said reliving the terrible experience in a book would be therapeutic and liberate him from the haunting nightmares. But he was careful not to become obsessive, unwilling to risk losing Akila a second time. He had learned a valuable lesson: Don't take your happiness and good fortune for granted. Enjoy every minute of it because, like a barely flickering flame, it could be snuffed instantaneously.

So his bond with Akila had grown. The relationship had become exciting and romantic—they were head-over-heels in love again. As the therapist had explained, "Figure out your desired outcome and then train your actions and words to acquire that outcome."

Pondering the thought, he realized he had achieved the desired outcome with respect to the omnipotent evil that wreaked havoc on PEI. But it had been at a terrible cost. When the smoke cleared, 27 people were dead, and 15 corpses had disappeared. Their remains had yet to be found.

Byron was grateful the tiny island was slowly returning to the pleasant, sleepy little province of old.

And grateful he had Akila back in one piece, although a little scarred physically and emotionally.

Lying on her back, she stared out at the waters, her slim orange bikini revealing plenty, while still leaving plenty to the imagination. He couldn't wait to get her inside the five-star hotel suite.

She looked contemplative. Now it was his turn. "What are you thinking about, honey?"

She turned, extracted a Presidente beer from a nearby cooler, and smiled, exposing brilliant white teeth.

He loved that smile.

"That I want a beer. Want one?"

"Sure."

They twisted the caps off, clinked glasses and drank.

"Cheers, baby," he said. "I love you."

She kissed him. "I love you too."

"Do you think we should go get the stragglers?" Byron asked.

"Why not? If we leave them too long they might end up fucking in the ocean."

"Yuck," Byron said, grinning wryly. "I don't want to swim in white goo."

Akila laughed, shaking her head.

Drinks in hand, they strode down to the water's edge, a fiery orange sliver of the setting sun visible in the distance.

Redmond and Susanne splashed each other playfully about twenty feet from shore.

Redmond had healed from the vicious attack. The panicked cries Byron had heard were not after all cries of death. He had suffered a head concussion as one of the beasts had throttled him and repeatedly slammed his head against a rock.

Susanne had also suffered a concussion, the result of an impromptu meeting with a baseball bat. She too had recovered, although at times she would gap out. Doctors said her brain might one day completely heal itself, but nobody really knew.

Only time would tell.

One thing for sure—Redmond and Susanne were getting along famously. There was a hint of a romance developing since their arrival at the resort three days ago. They were spending more and more time together. After all, they had something in common. They had both lost their respective spouses to tragic deaths.

Byron held up a beer. "Hey, you lovebirds, want a beer?"

They stopped splashing. Redmond looked at Susanne. She smiled and nodded.

"Sure," he said. "It's getting dark anyway. I plan on getting pissed after dinner, hit the disco. You guys into it?"

They nodded. Why not? They were on holiday. And Redmond was in a much better mood. He had finally gotten a well-deserved rest, after pushing himself right to the edge of a nervous breakdown.

Byron put an arm around Akila as they returned to the beach towel.

Redmond followed suit, putting a hand on Susanne's shoulder. She smiled.

As they walked, Byron glanced back at the ocean.

His jaw dropped.

Far away, glowing ominously on the water, was the fiery image of a phantom ship.

## Also by William Blackwell

*Phantom Rage, Poison Rage, Infected Rage*
*Nightmare's Edge*
*Resurrection Point*
*Brainstorm*
*Rule 14*
*Assaulted Souls*
*Assaulted Souls II*
*Assaulted Souls III*
*Blood Curse*
*Black Dawn*
*The Strap*
*The End is Nigh*
*Orgon Conclusion*
*Freaky Franky*
*The Witch's Tombstone*
*The Dark Menace*
*Tales of Damnation*
*In Your Dreams*
*Macabre Alley*
*A Head for an Eye*

### The *End is Nigh* Preview

Seven social outcasts flee bloodthirsty gangs and a fiery apocalypse.

"Love this book I've read it like a billion times." Goodreads

Cray Lenning's life as a garbage collector in a small town is reclusive and boring. Burdened with strong feelings of distrust and resentment, he's content to wallow in lonely self-pity. But when he witnesses a defrocked preacher proclaim "The end is nigh" seconds before getting struck by a car, Cray's world spirals out of control.

Initially, Cray dismisses the wayward preacher as a wacko, but ominous signs begin to convince him otherwise. Enter Sandra Colling, a heartbroken but resolute nurse. Together, they build an underground shelter to try and survive a deadly inferno blazing across the country, and embark on a frantic mission to save others.

Trapped inside the shelter, they learn the terrifying reality of their choices: a traumatized police detective; a manipulative and self-righteous psychologist; a sadomasochistic sex-addict; a rambling, alcoholic preacher; and a mentally ill redneck with an explosive temper.

Their dire predicament worsens when water runs out and they're forced to emerge from the shelter. To survive in this God-forsaken wasteland, they must form an unlikely alliance and battle a far more deadly presence topside—a gang of ruthless escaped convicts, hell-bent on starting an evil polygamist cult that rules by fear, intimidation, and brutal murder.

If you're a fan of Stephen King and Clive Barker, you'll love *The End is Nigh*, a riveting struggle for survival in a savage apocalyptic wasteland.

"Loved it, and highly recommend it." Amazon

"Underlying the strong plot line is vivid character development and intense examination of relationships and individual motivations." Goodreads

"This book kept me up all hours, until I had finished it! I could NOT put it down!!" Goodreads

## About the Author

Canadian dark fiction author William Blackwell studied journalism at Mount Royal University and English literature at The University of British Columbia.

He worked as a journalist and a newspaper editor for many years before pursuing his passion for storytelling. His novels have been characterized as graphic, edgy, and at times terrifying.

Currently living on a secluded acreage on Prince Edward Island, Blackwell finds much of his inspiration from Mother Nature, odd people, traveling, and bizarre nightmares.

## Author Comments

Thank you for reading this book. I would be eternally grateful if you would post a book review on your favorite book retailer website. A positive review is the highest compliment a writer can receive. Reviews are crucial to the success of any author. You don't have to say much. A few sentences will suffice.

Sign up for my newsletter if you want to be kept up to date on blog posts, new releases, and freebies. I promise I won't spam you and you can unsubscribe at any time.

Thanks again for your support.

http://www.wblackwell.com/free-ebook/